The Romance of Violette

by

Anonymous

[1891]

"A posthumous work by a celebrated incognito"

LOCUS ELM™

The Romance of Violette

by

Anonymous

(written 1891)

Originally published in by *The Erotica Biblion society of London and New York* in 1897

Published: August 2016

TABLE OF CONTENTS

PREFACE..7

CHAPTER 1...9

CHAPTER 2...16

CHAPTER 3...24

CHAPTER 4...29

CHAPTER 5...46

CHAPTER 6...53

CHAPTER 7...60

CHAPTER 8...68

CHAPTER 9...75

*

PREFACE

I have spent thousands of years in this earthly world, it would appear, and the spiritualistic component of my own being must have been successively transmitted in the continuity of human creatures, before it became my privilege to be one of the denizens of the planet of Mars, my present dwelling.

"How happy he will be," will exclaim those unfortunate mortals who still weep on earth, "for has he not left our vale of tears?"

No such thing! You are entirely mistaken, for I feel very dull here, in spite of the evident superiority, as a place of residence, of the planet I am now exploring.

Indeed, I frequently suffer from fits of depression, and often glance back longingly on a past which was not unmixed with bliss. That is why you behold me now with pen in hand, calling up the most pleasurable recollections of my earthly life and trying to retrace them to the reader.

I must own to many sins in the course of my terrestrial incarnations. My future readers will therefore understand why, among the outlines, which like dim shadows are evoked before my eyes, I look upon those of women with the most gratified feelings.

She who now receives my slumbering sensations, numbed, alas, by the ethereal poetry of the ambient atmosphere in which I breathe when on earth, went by euphonious name of Violette. She gave me all the joys of that paradise promised to the faithful by Mahomet, and when she died my grief was unspeakable.

Nobody now knows who was concealed under this pretty pseudonym. I may therefore freely pen her history, that of our loves! She had no other!

Before entrusting these sheets to the amorous zephyr which is to waft them on to the desk of some enterprising publisher, I would have my future readers know that they are not exactly suitable for young ladies.

And now, squeamish reader, and you, bashful lady, who are fearful of calling a spade a spade, you have had due warning; therefore tarry you a while, or else go no further, for these pages were not designed for you.

Let only those follow me, who understand love, and practise thy sweet science, O voluptas!

THE AUTHOR

CHAPTER 1

I was thirty years of age when I made the acquaintance of Violette.

I lived at the time on the fourth floor of a rather fine house in the Rue de Rivoli, just beneath rooms occupied by domestics and young girls employed in a linen drapery establishment on the ground floor under the arcades.

I was then on intimate terms with a very handsome and aristocratic lady. Her complexion was of that description which Theophile Gautier celebrates in his Emaux et Camees. Her hair was such as that with which Aeschylus adorns Electra's head and which compares to the fair corn of Argolide. But the lady had become rather too plump and stout at an early period of her career, and highly incensed at her premature embonpoint, displeased with herself and all the world, she worried all those who approached her, as if they should be made responsible for her misfortune.

As a consequence our intimacy went on the decline, and though I duly provided for all her wants and whims, I made no effort to bring into closer vicinity our respective bedchambers, situated at opposite ends of the suite of rooms. I had made choice of my own for the sake of the fine view on the Tuileries. I aspired already to be an author, and truly nothing can be finer, sweeter, more refreshing for a writer than the sight of this sombre mass of foliage formed by the ancient trees of the garden.

In summer the wood pigeons sport and frolic about the tall bough till twilight, when calm and silence begin to reign in their aerial abodes.

At ten o'clock the tattoo is heard and the gates are closed, and when the night is fine the moon slowly sails along the heavens, leaving its silvery track on the lofty tree tops.

Sometimes a light breeze makes the pale light tremble in the rustling leaves, which then seem to awaken, to live, and breathe of love and pleasure.

And by degrees, the noises of the big city grow more and more faint and distant to the ear which rests in the enjoyment of this delightful silence, while the eye gazes admiringly on the chateau and the dark, deep majestic masses of the huge trees. Often I would thus remain for hours at my window, dreaming and wrapped in thought.

What were the subjects of my dreams? I could hardly tell. I probably dreamt of what one dreams when one is thirty years of age; of love, of the women one has seen, and more often still, of those unseen as yet.

And in truth, are not the charms of the unknown fair ones the most potent of all?

There are men unfavoured by nature, whose hearts never thrill under a ray of sunlight. They live on as if in a kind of semi-darkness and accomplish as a duty, not as a joy, the act which is the supreme happiness of life, and which brings such rapture to the senses that if it lasted a minute instead of lasting five seconds it would kill even a Hercules.

These men in their passage through life, eat, drink and sleep; they indeed beget children, but they will never be able to say: "I have loved!" And surely is there anything worth living for, unless it be love?

I was wrapped in one of those dreams which have neither horizon nor limits, in which heaven and earth are mingled; I had just heard the bell in the neighbouring clock tower chime two o'clock, when I thought I heard a knock at my door. But perhaps I was mistaken, so I listened. The knock was repeated. Wondering who could come to visit me at this unwonted hour I ran to the door and opened it.

A young girl, almost a child slipped in and said:

"Oh, let me take refuge here, monsieur, I beseech you!"

I motioned her to be silent and softly shut the door. I then encircled her waist to my arm and took her to my bedroom. There I was enabled to have a view of the bird just escaped from its cage and which had flown to me for protection.

My supposition was correct; it was indeed a lovely girl, barely eighteen, straight and pliant as a reed, though her form already showed signs of womanhood.

I placed my hand on her bosom by chance, and I felt a living globe as firm as marble.

The mere contact sent a thrill through my veins. There are indeed women who have received from nature the fascinating gift of exciting sensual desires at the slightest touch.

"How frightened I was!" she murmured.

"Really?"

"Oh yes! How fortunate that you were not yet in bed!"

"And what was the cause of that great fright?"

"Monsieur Beruchet."

"Who is this Monsieur Beruchet?"

"The husband of the seamstress with whom I worked below."

"And pray tell me, what did this Monsieur Beruchet do to you?"

"But you will keep me all night, will you not?"

"I shall keep you as long as you like. It is not my custom to turn pretty girls out of doors."

"Oh, I am only a little girl. I am not a pretty girl."

"Well! well!" I gave a look at her bosom and what I saw through the half-opened chemise gave me reason to think she was not such a little girl as all that.

"Tomorrow, at break of day, I must go!" she murmured softly.

"And where will you go?"

"To my sister's."

"Your sister-and where does she live?"

"No. 4 Rue Chaptal."

"Your sister lives in the Rue Chaptal?"

"Yes, on the first floor. She has two rooms and will lend me one."

"And tell me, what is your sister doing in the Rue Chaptal?"

"She works for milliners' shops. Monsieur Ernest helps her."

"Is she older than you?"

"Yes, two years older."

"What is her name?"

"Marguerite."

"And what is yours?"

"Violette."

"It seems that in your family they were partial to the names of flowers."

"Oh yes, Mamma did like them so!"

"Is your mamma no more?"

"No, Monsieur."

"What was her name?"

"Rose."

"Well, they did like the names of flowers! And your father?"

"Oh, he is quite well."

"And what is his trade?"

"He is a keeper at the gates of Lille."

"What is his name?"

"Rouchat."

"But I perceive that I have been asking you questions for an hour, and I have not enquired of you why Monsieur Beruchet frightened you so?"

"Because he always tried to kiss me."

"You don't say so!"

"He followed me everywhere, and I never dared to go without a light into the back shop, because I was always sure of finding him there."

"Then you did not like him to kiss you?"

"Oh, not at all!"

"And why were you displeased so?"

"Because he is so ugly, and then I thought he did not only want to kiss me."

"But what did he want else?"

"I don't know."

I looked at her to see whether she wasn't making fun of me. But I perceived from her innocent look, that she was perfectly in earnest.

"Well, then, what did he do, besides kissing you?"

"He came up to my room yesterday when I was in bed; at least I think it was he, and he tried to open my door."

"Did he say anything?"

"No, but during the day, he said: 'Do not shut your door as you did yesterday, little one, I have something of importance to tell you.'"

"And you locked your door all the same."

"Oh, yes I did. More securely than ever."

"Did he come?"

"Yes, he did come. He tried all he could to open the door. He tapped and tapped; then he knocked louder. Then he said 'It is I, little Violette'. You may well imagine that I gave no reply. I was shaking with fright in my bed. The more he said, 'It is I', the more he called me darling Violette, the more I put my blanket over my head. At last after waiting at least half an hour, he went away grumbling."

"All day he looked sulky so that I was in hopes he would leave me alone tonight. I was half undressed, as you see me, when I thought of bolting the door. But the bolt had been taken off during the day and there was no lock there; so, without losing a moment I ran off and knocked at your door. Oh! how lucky I did so!" And the child threw her arms around my neck.

"So you're not frightened of me?"

"Oh, no!"

"And if I wished to kiss you, would you run away?"

"See now," said she, and she applied her humid and fresh mouth to my parched lips.

I could not help keeping my lips on hers for a few seconds while I caressed her teeth with the tip of my tongue. She closed her eyes and leaned her head backwards, saying: "Oh, how nice, is that kind of kiss!"

"You've never been kissed that way?" I inquired.

"No," she said, passing her tongue over her burning lips. "Is it the usual way?"

"Yes, when you love the person."

"Then, you do love me?"

"If I am not yet in love with you I am afraid I soon shall be."

"Just like me!"

"So much the better!"

"And what do people do who love one another?"

"They exchange kisses as we just have done."

"Is that all?"

"Yes."

"Well, that is funny. It seemed to me I wished for something else; as if this kiss, however sweet it may be, were only the beginning of love."

"What did you feel?"

"I cannot say; a kind of languid sensation in all my body. A pleasure such as I have experienced sometimes in dreams."

"And when you awoke after these dreams, how did you feel?"

"I was quite exhausted."

"Did you never have that sensation except in a dream?"

"Yes, indeed, just now, when you kissed me."

"Am I then the first man who ever kissed you?"

"In that way, you are. My father often kissed me, but it was not at all the same thing."

"Then you are still a virgin?"

"Virgin, what does that mean?" Evidently, from her tone she was sincere!

I took pity, or rather I felt respect for that innocence which then put itself so entirely at my mercy. It seemed as if it were a crime to rob her of that sweet treasure, which she unconsciously possessed, and which, when once given away, is lost forever.

"And now let us talk seriously, my dear girl," I said, releasing her from my embrace.

"Oh, you are not going to send me away, surely?"

"No, I am too happy to have you here." Then, after a pause: "Listen," I said, "this is what we are going to do. We will go and fetch your clothes."

"Very well, and where shall I go?"

"That's my business. First of all let us go to your room."

"And Monsieur Beruchet?"

"It is probable that he has left, for it is nearly three o'clock in the morning."

"What shall we do in my room?"

"We will take away all your things."

"And then?"

"And then I shall take you with your little luggage to a room in town, whence you will write to Monsieur Beruchet a letter which I shall dictate. Are you willing?"

"Oh, I shall do as you bid me."

How charming this confidence of innocence and youth! The darling girl, she would certainly have done all I bade her, there and then.

We went up to the lockless room, and put her scanty belongings into a carpetbag.

Violette finished dressing herself, we came downstairs, and, as there were no cabs about, we set out arm in arm, as happy and light-hearted as two school chums, repaired to the Rue Saint Augustin, where I kept a room for a night's debauch when I felt so inclined.

An hour later I was home again, without having tried to make further progress in my amours with Violette.

CHAPTER 2

The room which I kept in the Rue Saint Augustin was not in a lodging house. It was a room which I had furnished myself, in view of its destination, with such taste as would have satisfied the most dainty lady.

It was hung all around in carnation velvet; the window curtains and bed curtains were of the same material. The bed was covered with velvet also, and the whole set off by Torsells and bands of gold satin.

A looking glass occupied the whole of the wall inside the bed and corresponded with the mirror placed between the two windows so that images were reproduced ad infinitum.

The rest of the furniture was in keeping with this elegant decoration. A bath was hidden in a sofa and a large bearskin made the pretty feet which rested on it look still whiter.

A pretty little lady's maid, whose only functions were to keep the room in order and to attend to the different lady visitors, had her room on the same landing.

I bade her prepare a bath in the dressing room without awaking the occupant of the bedroom.

We entered without a light, and only lit a night lamp in a vase of rose coloured Bohemian glass. Then I turned away to allow the young girl to undress freely, an operation which in her innocence she would have done in my presence. After which I kissed her on both eyes, bade her good night and returned home as I said before.

In spite of the emotions of the day, Violette went to bed, where she nestled like a little pussy. She said goodbye with a yawn, and I am sure she must have been fast asleep before I was well in the street.

As for me, the case was different, and I could not close my eyes. I confess-that bosom from which my hand had rebounded, that mouth which had been glued to my lips that half opened chemise which had disclosed such lovely treasures-the recollection kept me awake and in a state of great excitement.

I am certain male readers will not ask for any explanation of my conduct, for they fully understand why I stopped half way.

But lady readers more inquisitive or more ignorant of certain articles of our code, will surely wish to know why I went no further.

I must say that it was not for lack of desire, but Violette, as I stated before, was barely eighteen years old, and then she was so innocent that it would have seemed like a crime to take possession of charms given away, so to speak, without any consciousness of the seriousness of the act. And again, I must add, that I am one of those who delight in the relish of all the preliminary delicacies of love, all the voluptuousness of its most complicated pleasures.

Innocence is a flower which should be left unculled as long as possible on its stalk, and should be plucked only leaf by leaf.

A rosebud will sometimes be a week in bursting into a full blown flower. Besides, I like pleasure without attendant remorse; and within the walls of the city which so well defended itself against the invader in 1792 there existed a veteran whose old age I respected.

The worthy man did not seem as if he would have committed suicide on account of the mishap of his eldest daughter, but perhaps he loved more tenderly his youngest-perhaps he had formed for her future plans which I did not like to upset. Besides, I have always noticed that with patience everything goes well for everybody.

I thus pondered until daybreak. Pent up with fatigue, I at last closed my eyes and slept on till eight o'clock.

I got up hastily, as Violette must have been an early riser. I told my man that I should probably not be home for breakfast, I hailed a cab, and in five minutes was at the house in Rue Saint Augustin.

I went upstairs four steps at a time, and my heart beat as if this were my first love.

I entered the room noiselessly. Not only was Violette fast asleep, but she had not even moved.

However, the blankets were partly drawn back, and, as her chemise was half opened, one of her breasts was exposed to my view.

She was charming thus, with her head thrown back and nearly hidden by her luxuriant locks; then she looked like a picture by Giorgione.

Her bosom was marvellously plump and as white as snow. Though a brunette, the nipples of her breasts were rose and like strawberries. I leaned over and applied my lips lightly to one of them; it stiffened instantly, whilst a slight shudder ran through her frame. Had I only chosen to pull off the sheets, I am sure she would not have opened her eyes.

But I preferred awaiting the close of her slumbers. I took a seat near the bed and held one of her hands in mine.

By the light of the night lamp I examined that hand; it was small, of a comely shape, rather short like the hands of Spaniards, and the nails were rosy, pointed, but the forefinger bore evidence of needlework. While I was thus employed she suddenly opened her eyes and uttered a joyful exclamation.

"Oh!" she said, "you are here, how happy I am! If I had not seen you on waking up I should have thought it was all a dream. Did you never leave me then?"

"I did," I replied, "I left you for four or five hours, which seemed like ages, but I returned, hoping to be the first object on which you should set eycs on waking up."

"And how long have you been here?"

"For half an hour."

"You should have woke me."

"I should never have thought of doing so."

"You did not even kiss me!"

"Yes, I did, I kissed one of your pretty little rosebuds."

"Which?"

"The one on the left."

She uncovered it with a genuine air of innocence and tried to touch it with her lips.

"Oh, how tiresome!" said she. "I cannot kiss it in my turn."

"And why should you like to kiss it in your turn?"

"To place my lips where yours have lain."

She renewed the attempt.

"I can do it! Well," she said, "you gave it a kiss just now for your own sake, let your lips touch it now for my sake."

Thereupon I leant over her and taking the rosebud between my lips I caressed it with the tip of my tongue.

She gave a little cry of pleasure:

"Oh, how nice!"

"As nice as yesterday's kiss?"

"Oh! yesterday's kiss. It is so long since, I cannot remember."

"Shall I begin again?"

"You know I should like you to, since you told me that was the proper way to kiss people you loved."

"But I don't know yet whether I love you."

"As for me, I am quite sure that I do love you dearly. So do not kiss me if you don't like to do it, but I shall kiss you all the same."

And as on the previous day she glued her lips to mine, with this difference, that this time her tongue touched my teeth.

I could not have got away had I wished to do so, she hugged me so tightly.

Her head fell back and with half closed eyes she murmured:

"Oh, how I love you!"

The kiss made me mad; I snatched her, so to speak, from the bed, and pressing her closely to my heart I covered her bosom with kisses.

"Oh, what are you doing, I feel quite faint?"

These words brought me to my senses, for it was not thus, by surprise, that I wished to possess her.

"Dear girl," said I, "I have had a bath got ready for you in the dressing room." With these words I carried her there in my arms.

"Ah!" said she, sighing, "how comfortable I feel in your arms."

The bath was just warm enough, I put her into it after having poured in half a bottle of eau-de-Cologne. I then lit the fire and placed the bearskin rug in front of it.

Then I brought out a dressing gown of white cashmere and put before an armchair a pair of small red Turkish slippers with gold embroidery.

After a quarter of an hour, my little bather came out quite shivering and ran to the fire.

"Oh, how nice and warm!" she said, and she sat on the (bearskin at my feet.

She was charming in her cambric peignoir of such transparent texture that the skin could be seen through it. She looked round and said:

"Dear me, how pretty everything is here. Am I to live in this place?"

"Yes, if you like, but we must have somebody's permission."

"Whose?"

"Your father's."

"My father's! But will he not be glad when he knows I have a beautiful room and plenty of leisure time for study?"

"To study what?"

"Ah! I had forgotten. I must explain."

"Do, my dear girl, by all means. You know you must tell me all," said I, kissing her.

"You remember one day you gave me a ticket for a play?"

"Yes, I do remember."

"It was for the Porte-Saint-Martin theatre, where they played Antony, by M. Dumas."

"It is an immoral play, not at all fit for young girls to see."

"I did not think so at all. I was quite taken up with it, and ever since that day, I told my sister and Monsieur Ernest that I wished to appear on the stage."

"You don't say so?"

"Then Monsieur Ernest and my sister exchanged glances. 'Well,' said my sister, 'if she has any taste at all for it, it would be preferable to the milliner's business."

"'And then,' said Monsieur Ernest, With my journal, the Gazette des Theatres, I can give her a lift."

"'Well, that will be just the thing for her.'"

"Madame Beruchet was told that I should sleep at my sister's and that I should not return until next day. After the play we returned to the Rue Ghaptal and I began to repeat the principal scenes which I remembered, and I set to acting all the while moving my arms about like this-"

But meanwhile Violette unconsciously had opened her peignoir and disclosed some lovely treasures to my view.

I took her in my arms, set her on my knee, and she nestled lovingly against me.

"What next?" I asked.

"Monsieur Ernest then said that if my mind was made up, as two or three years must elapse before I made my debut, I must let my father know of the plan."

"'And during these two or three years, how will she live?' asked Marguerite.

"'What a question to ask!' replied Monsieur Ernest. 'She is pretty and a pretty girl need not want for anything. From eighteen to eighteen she will find a protector. Besides she eats no more than a little bird. What does she require? A nest and a little seed.' "

I shrugged my shoulders while casting a glance at the poor little creature nestling in my arms as in a cradle.

"Then," resumed Violette, "the next day they wrote to Papa."

"And what did Papa reply?"

"He replied: 'You are two poor orphans thrown upon the world without any other protector than an old man of sixty-seven who may at any moment be taken away from you. Therefore, do the best you can, but never do anything which would make the poor old soldier ashamed of you.'"

"Did you keep that letter?"

"Yes, I did."

"Where is it?"

"In the pocket of one of my gowns. Then I thought of you. I said: 'Since he gave me tickets for the play, he must be acquainted with the managers of theatres.' I always put it off till the next day. But the affair with Monsieur Beruchet decided it all. Will you do all you can to help me in studying for the stage?"

"I will indeed, I promise you."

"How good you are." And Violette threw her arms round my neck, and so doing laid bare the treasures of her bosom.

This time, I confess, I lost my head; my hand glided down her body and rested upon a spot covered with hair as soft and as fine as silk.

When Violette felt my hand her whole body seemed to vibrate; her head fell back, her mouth was half opened, while her eyes were nearly closed. And yet, I had hardly touched her.

I was mad with passion and carrying her to the bed, I knelt before her and placed my mouth where my hand had been. I experienced then the supreme pleasure of one's lips in contact with virginity.

From this moment, Violette uttered inarticulate words, till a spasm of pleasure thrilled through her whole body.

I got up and gazed on her while she was recovering. She opened her eyes, tried to sit up, and murmured:

"Oh, how delicious it was! Can we begin again?"

Suddenly she got up and looking intently at me, she asked:

"Is it not very wicked?"

I sat near her on the bed.

"Has anybody ever spoken to you seriously?"

"Yes, sometimes father did, when I was a child, to scold me."

"I don't mean that. I mean to ask you whether you could understand anyone who should talk to you seriously?"

"Not perhaps if it were a stranger. But I believe I can understand anything you say to me."

"Well then, listen."

She clasped her arms round my neck, fixed her eyes on mine and with an attentive air, said: "Now speak, I listen."

"Woman, when created, certainly received the same rights as a man, that is, the right of obeying one's natural instincts.

"Well, society being ruled by men, who are stronger than women, certain laws have been forced on women. Chastity is imposed on girls, and fidelity on married women.

"Men, in framing these laws, have reserved for themselves the right of satisfying their passions, without thinking that in order to indulge them they must cause women to break the laws they laid down for them.

"These women give them happiness, but shame is their own lot."

"That is very unjust!" remarked Violette.

"Yes, my dear, truly so. Therefore have certain women risen up and said: "What does society offer me in exchange for the bondage in which she keeps me? Marriage with a man I shall not probably love, who will take me at eighteen years of age, who will enjoy me and make me unhappy all my life. I had rather remain outside of society, follow my own inclinations and love whom I please. I shall be a woman of nature, not of society.

"From society's conventional point of view, what we have done was wrong. From nature's point of view, we have only given satisfaction to our legitimate desires."

"Did you understand?"

"Quite well."

"Well, think of this all day. This evening you can let me know whether you want to be nature's woman or that of society."

I rang the bell and the maid came. Violette was in her bed, showing only her head. "Madame Leonie," I said, "you will please attend to all this young lady's wants; you will have her food sent by Chevet, her pastry from Julien's. There is Bordeaux wine in the cupboard and 300 francs in this drawer.

"Ah! I forgot. Send for a dressmaker to measure the young lady for two simple but tasteful dresses, with bonnets to match."

When I returned in the evening, Violette ran up to me, and, throwing herself into my arms, she said:

"I thought of what you told me."

"All day?"

"No, for five minutes, and I prefer to be nature's woman."

"You do not wish to return to Monsieur Beruchet?"

"Oh, no!"

"You wish to return to your sister's?"

Violette made no reply.

"Do you think it inconvenient to return to your sister's?"

"I am afraid it may not please Monsieur Ernest."

"Who is that Monsieur Ernest?"

"A young man who visits my sister and who is a journalist."

"What makes you think that he would not like to see you with your sister?"

"Because, when by chance Madame Beruchet sent me for an errand, and I quickly ran to kiss my sister when M. Ernest was there, he looked quite sulky. He went into the other room with Marguerite and locked the door. One day I remained because the lady had told me to wait for an answer and that seemed to put them both out of temper."

"Well, then there is an end of it, you shall be the woman of nature."

CHAPTER 3

Dear girl! It was indeed nature, but a delightful nature which inspired her.

I had some excellent books in my library. She had been reading all day.

"Did you feel dull?" I asked.

"Yes, on account of your absence, but not otherwise."

"What did you read?"

"I read *Valentine*."

"Then I am not surprised," I replied. "That book is a masterpiece."

"I do not know. But what I do know is that it made me cry all the time."

I rang the bell for Madame Leonie.

"Get tea ready," I said. Then I asked Violette: "Do you like tea?"

"I don't know. I never tasted it."

When tea was ready, I asked Violette whether she required the service of Leonie any longer. She said, "No" so I shut the door and locked it.

"Are you going to remain here?"

"If you will allow me."

"All night?"

"All night!"

"Oh, won't that be nice! Then we can go to bed like two good little friends."

"Just so. Have you ever slept with any of your girl friends?"

"At school, when I was quite little; but not since then, except when I slept with my sister."

"What did you do then?"

"I used to say good night; I kissed her, and we both went to sleep.
"That is all."

"And if we slept together, do you think that would be all?"

"I hardly know; but it seems to me there should be something else."

"But then, what could we do together?"

She shrugged her shoulders. "Perhaps what you did to me this morning," she said, embracing me.

I took her in my arms and put her on my knees. She was silent for some time; then she smiled and said:

"Can you guess what I should like?"

"No."

"I should like to be learned."

"Learned! Why would you like to be learned, of all things in the world?"

"To understand what I do not understand."

"What is it you do not understand?"

"A good many things. For instance you asked me whether I was a virgin."

"Yes."

"Well, I replied, I did not know, and you burst out laughing."

"That is correct."

"Well, what is it to be a virgin?"

"A virgin is a young lady who has never been caressed by a man."

"Then I am no longer a virgin now?"

"How's that?"

"Why, it seems to me that you caressed me this morning."

"But there are different ways of caressing, my dear girl. The kisses I gave you this morning, though very sweet..."

"Oh, yes, they were sweet! They were indeed!"

"However sweet, they do not destroy virginity."

"And what are those that do take away one's virginity?"

"I should first explain to you what is virginity."

"Do explain it to me, then."

"It is no easy matter."

"Oh no, you are so clever!"

"Well, virginity is the physical and moral state of a girl who, like you, has not had a lover."

"But what is having a lover?"

"It is doing with a man certain things by which children are begotten and brought into the world."

"Did we not do these things?"

"No!"

"Then you are not my lover?"

"I am only as yet your sweetheart."

"When will you be my lover?"

"In as long a time as possible."

"I suppose it is because you would dislike it?"

"Not at all, just the reverse. It is the thing that I should like above all things in the world."

"Oh dear! how tiresome! I no longer understand you."

"To be the lover of a woman, pretty little Violette, is to be, in the alphabet of love's pleasures, at the letter Z of the ordinary alphabet. There are twenty-four letters to learn before you come to the end of that series whose first letter, the letter A, is a kiss on the hand."

I took her little hand and kissed it.

"And what you did to me this morning-what letter was it?"

I was fain to confess that it stood very close to letter Z, and that I had omitted many vowels and consonants to get to that stage.

"You are chaffing me!"

"No, indeed I am not, sweet darling. I should like to make this alphabet last as long as possible-this charming alphabet of love, of which each letter is a caress and each caress is bliss. I should wish to take off little by little that robe of innocence, just as I shall pluck one by one all the different articles of your apparel from your person.

"If you were dressed, each portion that I should take off would disclose something new to me-something unknown, something charming; the neck, the shoulder, the bosom, and, by degrees, all the rest. Like a brute, I divested you of all in a moment. You did not know the value of all that you gave away."

"Then I have done wrong?"

"No, no! I loved you too much, too passionately, to proceed otherwise."

I slipped off her gown, and then she sat on my knee clad only in her chemise.

"You wish to know what is virginity," I said, losing all control of

26

myself. "Well, I wall tell you; but draw near-nearer still-your lips on mine."

I pressed her to my breast; she clasped her arms round my neck, sighing and panting with amorous excitement.

"Do you feel my hand?" I asked.

"Oh, yes!" said she, with a shiver through her whole frame.

"And my finger, do you feel it too?"

"Yes.... Yes!..."

"I am now touching what they call the maidenhead. When once this is broken through you cease to be a virgin, and you become a woman. Well, what I wish is to caress you only in such a way that you shall keep that maidenhead as long as possible. Do you understand?"

Directly my finger was fixed there, Violette gave no other answer than by caressing me fondly and muttering passionate words. Then she entwined her body round mine, uttered inarticulate exclamations, sighed, and suddenly she loosened her hold of me; her head fell back, and she lay as if in a swoon. I undressed rapidly, tore off her chemise, and stretched her against me in the bed.

She soon recovered and said:

"Oh, I am dead!"

"Dead!" I cried. "You dead! Just as if you said I was dead. Oh, no! on the contrary, we are beginning to live." And I covered her with kisses which made her writhe as if they had been so many bites. Then she began in her turn to bite me with little passionate cries. Each time our lips met there was a pause, full of voluptuous pleasure.

Suddenly she gave a cry of astonishment, and seized with both hands the unknown object which had caused her surprise, as if the veil were torn asunder.

"I understand," said she, "it is with this-But it is quite impossible."

"Violette, my sweet darling, I can no longer restrain myself; I shall become mad!"

I tried to tear myself away from her embraces.

"No," she said. "Remain if you love me. Do not be afraid of hurting me, I wish it."

She then slipped under me, clasped her arms around my neck, twined her thighs round mine, pushing her body against my own.

"I wish it," she repeated-"I wish it."

Suddenly she gave a little shriek.

All my fine resolutions had vanished. At the same time that Violette began to understand what was a maidenhead, she had lost her own.

On hearing her cry out, I stopped.

"Oh, no" she said, "go on!... go on!... You hurt me; but if you did not hurt me, I should be too happy! I wish to have pain! Go, do not stop! Do, dear Christian, my beloved! my friend! Oh, I shall go mad!

"Oh, it is like fire! Oh, I die!

"Take me, take all!"

Ah! Mahomet fully knew by what dream he should enthral man when he gave his disciples the sensual Paradise-a bottomless abyss of voluptuous rapture always renewed.

We spent a night full of bliss-of passionate caresses, and never closed eyes till day break.

"Ah!" said she, on waking and embracing me, "I hope now I am no longer a virgin."

CHAPTER 4

The pain which poor Violette had suffered was not serious; but it was irritating when not counteracted by love's pleasures. I told her before leaving that she should bathe the injured parts in bran water, with an application of a decoction of marshmallow.

I had to explain to her the anatomy of the parts under treatment, and, with the aid of a looking glass, and thanks to the pliancy of her body, I was able to make the demonstration on her own person.

Violette, in her innocence, had never thought of looking at herself and what she saw was perfectly unknown to her.

During the night we spent together she had acquired some vague notions on the way of begetting children. I began by explaining to her the general and physical effect of nature, which is the reproduction of the human kind, the perfecting of this species being quite a secondary matter, a detail of society.

I further pointed out that it was solely with that object that nature had ordained such rapturous sensations in the conjunctions of the sexes, and that the certainty of eternal victory of life over death rested entirely in the attraction which was experienced by all living things, from man to plants.

Then I went into details and explained to her the part played by each organ. I began with the clitoris, the seat of pleasure in young girls, and which is so little developed with them. I then passed on to the membrane of Hymen, thrown as a veil of modesty on the vagina, which later on becomes the maternal outlet. In short, I disclosed to her all the mysteries of the organs of procreation.

She listened with the utmost attention and seemed to drink in all my words, which impressed themselves one by one on her memory.

After this I left her dreaming and pondering over all that I had told her, and wondering that so many things should be concealed by the veil of her innocence.

My resolve was to devote my spare time to Violette's company, but not to neglect meanwhile my usual labours. The lectures which I attended at the School of Medicine, and studies at different museums, always took place in the daytime, I could therefore very well manage to carry them on concurrently with my nocturnal occupations at the Rue Saint Augustin.

When I returned that evening to Violette's room, I found the tea all ready, with cakes and other delicacies. In my absence, Violette had performed her duties as mistress of the house. We therefore dismissed Leonie, with those services we could very well dispense.

We were once more alone. I had left with Violette the preceding evening, a copy of a letter for M. Beruchet. She had written it and forwarded it; there was nothing further to be done in that quarter, and we might rest in peace. No unpleasant enquiries or researches would now be made on account of Violette's sudden disappearance.

She had been too busy thinking to feel dull. All I had told her made an impression on her mind, and she had been pondering on the mysteries I had disclosed. Then, her curiosity being awakened, she had divested herself of all her garments, lighted the candles, and minutely examined her person. But as she had never seen any other woman naked she could not judge the degree of perfection or imperfection of the different parts of her form. Getting tired of this examination, she had set herself to read, but as chance would have it, the book she had taken up was just the sort of book that would set her mind to working. She was in an utter state of perplexity, for the work she was perusing was, Mademoiselle de Maupin by Theophile Gautier.

Now Mademoiselle de Maupin, in the garb of a dashing cavalier, made love to a young lady, and the intrigue wound up by one of those enigmatical scenes of which only a perfect knowledge of the ways of ancient civilization could furnish any clue.

This was the very scene that made poor Violette wonder so. I explained that, in the same way that among molluscs and plants hermaphrodites are to be found (or beings possessing either sex) there were in the animal kingdom, on woman especially, instances of bisexual organs, in appearance at least, on account of the large proportions of the clitoris. I told her that the Greeks, great worshippers, or rather fanatics, of physical beauty, with the view of creating beauteous forms not existing in nature, supposed that the son of Mercury and Venus had been seen bathing in the waters of a fountain, by the nymph Salamacis, who begged the gods to unite her body to that of her lover. The gods granted her prayer, and from the adjunction of female beauty to male beauty there sprang a creature with both sexes, experiencing the same amorous desires for man or woman, and able to satisfy them in both ways.

I promised to take her to the museum to see the Hermaphrodite of Farnese, which, reclining in an easy position on a couch, combines in his person the beauty of both man and woman.

But I explained that this perfect distinction of sexes did not exist in nature, though it is a fact that women with an elongated clitoris often have a marked penchant for persons of their own sex. This was an occasion for relating the story of Sappho, the founder of that worship which, though established hundreds of years ago, has still so many disciples in modern society.

I told her there were two Sapphos-one from Eresas, the other from Mitylene; the one a courtesan, the other a priestess; the one of perfect beauty, the other of ordinary attractions. The adoration of the Greeks for beauty was so great that they struck medals representing the courtesan of Eresas as though she had been a queen.

The other, the Sappho of Mitylene, the less attractive, had reached the marriageable age without having loved or being loved, and she resolved, in imitation of the Amazons of old, to form a league against men, but this new league was still more complete, insomuch that once a year the Amazons allowed their husbands to visit them in their island, whereas the disciples of Sappho made the vow to keep aloof altogether from males, and to have lovers none but persons of their own sex.

"But," asked Violette, innocently, "what can women do together?"

"They can do what I did to you the day before yesterday with finger and tongue; besides, the name which was given them explains the arts to which they give themselves up. They are called Tribades, from a verb which signifies to rub."

Sappho moreover, invented an instrument made of certain materials which in shape and appearance resembled the virile member.

Ezekiel, who lived three hundred years after Sappho, reproached the women of Jerusalem with making use of these kinds of images made of gold and silver.

The scandal caused by Sappho grew to such proportions that Venus thought it high time to put an end to it, the more so as the Lesbian religion was being propagated to the other islands of Greece, and, in consequence, her altars were in danger of being left without worshippers.

There existed a handsome ferryman named Phon, who took passengers from one shore to the other in the harbour of Mitylene. She disguised herself as an old beggar woman, and asked the ferryman to take her over free of charge. But on reaching the opposite bank it so happened that Phon became aware that his passenger was not an old beggar woman, but the goddess of Beauty and Love.

The sight of Venus produced so potential and visible an effect upon the handsome boatman that it would have been ungrateful on her part not to grant him a reward. Venus therefore blew all round them a cloud which enveloped and hid them from view.

After an hour the cloud was wafted away. Phon found himself alone, but Venus had presented him with a certain perfumed oil which, when applied to his person, would make him loved by all women.

Phon, of course, did not fail to make use of his oil, and as Sappho, when passing him by chance, inhaled the perfume from his locks, she fell in love with handsome Phon, and loved him as she was capable of loving, that is, madly.

Phon jilted her. This was the revenge of the goddess. Seeing that Phon was not to be won, and not being able to renew the miracle of Samilies, Sappho proceeded to Leucate to leap off the rock.

"Why should she jump off a rock?" asked Violette.

"Because disappointed lovers who leaped from the rock into the sea were cured if they could safely reach the bank; if drowned, the cure was still more complete."

"And do you say there are such women?"

"Many."

"Wait a little."

"What?"

"I remember-"

"Ah, I suppose some fair lady fell in love with you."

"Well, I believe that may be the case."

"'Pon my word, it would be an amusing thing. Tell me all about it."

She settled down on my knees.

"Well," she said, "when I was at Madame Beruchet's, there came sometimes in a fine carriage and pair, with a black footman, a great lady whom they called Madame la Comtesse. When she bought corsets, or dressing gowns or drawers, she would have me in the back shop, to see that the articles fitted her.

"At first she did not pay more attention to me than to the others, but by degrees, it seemed to her that nothing she bought would suit her unless it passed through my hands; so much so that she would buy any article offered to her as my own make, though I had never touched it.

"Four days ago-but you will see I had never given any thought to it at the time, but I remember now-they had some goods to be delivered to her, and she sent her carriage saying that I, and no other girl, should take them to her. I went and found her alone in a small boudoir hung with satin, and a quantity of vases and beautiful china about. The lady's maid was there and asked whether she should wait on her, but the Comtesse dismissed her, saying she would not for the time require her services. Indeed, when we were alone, she said it was all very well, but I must try on myself all the articles ordered, because if she tried them on she would never be able to tell whether they fitted.

"I pointed out that I was shorter by a head, and that consequently, it would be impossible to know how they would fit her; but she would not hear me, and began to undress me.

"I offered no resistance though I was quite ashamed, and I dared not open my lips while she divested me of my kerchief and my bodice, exclaiming the while: 'Oh! the pretty neck! Ah! what beautiful shoulders! What charming little bubbles!' and she kissed my neck, my throat and bosom, passing her hands all over and her lips afterwards. Suddenly she said: 'But I forgot, you must try on the drawers.'

"They were pretty drawers with embroidery. She pulled off mine by putting her hands under my chemise, and said: 'Why, her skin is really like satin!'

"'You must one day take a bath with me, will you not? pretty darling, and I will rub you with almond paste and you will become as white as ermine; and, besides, you will have a pretty little black tail, like an ermine.' Saying this, she tried to put her hand on my hair, but I made a spring backwards.

"'Why, you little wild thing, what is the matter with you? Why do you shrink away from me? Do I frighten you?' then she embraced me; but seeing my blushes and perceiving that I was trembling all over, no doubt she dared not push matters further, as she said: 'Come, try that on yourself,' I tried the drawers on. They were too large and too long for me. That gave her a pretext for passing her hands up my thighs in order to pull them up. For a moment her hand remained motionless, or I should say rather that it moved up and down gently so that it seemed as if it were trembling.

"Finally, when she had well kissed me, caressed me, and felt me all over, 'Oh!' she said, 'I think they will fit beautifully. In fact I am sure.'

"Then she dressed me herself, caressing me the while as (before. At last, just before I left, she whispered in my ear:

"'Do not forget that next Sunday you will spend all day with me, that we will take a bath together, and that we dine and go to the theatre together. Mind you, dress yourself prettily. I shall call for you in the afternoon about two o'clock.'"

"But, Sunday is tomorrow!"

"Well, she will not find me at the shop, that's all!"

"How is it you did not breathe a word of all this business?"

"So many things have happened to me during the last few days that I have not even thought of the Comtesse. What a disappointment for her!" and with these words the little romp clapped her hands.

A thought suddenly struck me.

"Would you be afraid if a woman made love to you?"

"I! What should I be afraid of?"

"I don't know."

"No; especially if I am forewarned and I know what it is. Come, you have formed some plan?"

34

"I? No, I confess, however, that I should feel amused to see how a woman sets about it, to make love to another woman."

"Just, as if you hadn't seen that already, you wicked man!"

"No, I once saw some girls playing at that sort of thing for the sake of money; but you know, it was not the real thing."

"Well, that is a pity."

"Perhaps it would be possible to renew your acquaintance with her?"

"How?"

"Do you know her address?"

"No."

"But you were at her house."

"The carriage took me there, but I did not notice the street or number."

"If such is the case let us say no more about it. You will find some other lady-love, perhaps more than one-I feel certain."

"Well, now when I come to think of it, you are not jealous, sir?"

"Of a woman, why should I be jealous of a woman? She will only excite your amorous desires, and I shall get a much better reception when I come to satisfy them."

"But if it were a man?"

"Ah!" said I, in as serious a tone as I could; "that's another matter. If you deceived me with a man, I should kill you!"

"I am glad to hear that. I was getting afraid that you did not love me."

"Do not love you? You will see!" Luckily it was easy for me to give her proofs of my love. I took her in my arms and put her on the bed. In a moment we lay stark naked side by side.

I had forgotten till then to pull aside the curtain which hid the looking glass, I slipped the cord and it came into view.

Violette uttered an exclamation of joy.

"Ah!" said she, "how charming. We shall be able to see ourselves in the glass."

"Yes; as long as you can look on."

"I bet you I will look to the very end."

"I bet you cannot."

I began operations by imprinting a long kiss on that part called the Mount of Venus.

"Ah!" said she, "you will not be able to see anything now."

"You will use your eyes for both of us, and I will guess as much as I can."

I then used my tongue as I had done before.

"Ah!" she said, "I know what you are doing; but the sensation is even better than the other day. Oh! where do you put your tongue now? The sensation is so delightful, I think I shall die!... Good gracious!... No! no! I will not yield! I will resist!... I will... Ah I am vanquished!... My dear love, my eyes are closing up... I cannot see anything. I die!"

Nights follow one another without being alike for lovers only, but as the description of this one might seem the exact reproduction of the preceding one, I shall beg leave of the reader to say nothing further about it.

The next day about twelve o'clock, I was drawing a sketch of Violette from memory, when there came a ring at the bell, and my servant said the Comtesse de Mainfoy wished to see me. I had a foreboding.

"Usher her in," I said to my man, and going to the door of the dining room, I led the way to my bedroom, which served me also for a study and a studio.

She seemed at first a little embarrassed, took an armchair and after some hesitation lifted her veil. She was a tall young woman of about eight and twenty, with magnificent curls flowing over her shoulders; her eyebrows, eyelashes and eyes were jet black, her nose straight, her lips as red as coral, with a rather heavy chin. Her breasts and hips were not so well developed as one might have expected from her height.

Perceiving that I awaited an explanation of her visit:

"Sir," she said, "you will perhaps think it rather strange that I should call on you; but you alone can give me the information I seek."

I bowed assent.

"I am too happy, Madame, to be able to do anything for you."

"Sir, there was at the milliner's who lives on the ground floor of this house, a young girl who goes by the name of Violette."

"Just so, Madame."

"She disappeared three days ago. When I enquired of her young friends and the mistress of the house, they one and all replied that they could not say what had become of her. But when I applied to the master and said that I felt much interested in the child; in fact, to a degree that I should employ the police to look for her, he said that he had good reasons for believing that if I applied to you, I could procure the information I require. I trust therefore, you will kindly inform me of her whereabouts."

"I have no reason whatever for keeping the child out of the way, especially as you wish her well; but I was wrong no doubt in keeping her from M. Beruchet, who had unscrewed the bolt of her bedroom so as to be able to enter at any time for his own purposes. At two o'clock in the morning the child came here for protection, and I took her in, that's all."

"What! is she here?" cried the Comtesse.

"Not here, Madame; that was impossible. But I had my own bachelor's rooms where I took her."

"Will you kindly let me have the address?"

"With the greatest of pleasure, Madame. Violette has often spoken of you."

"She spoke to you about me?"

"Yes, Madame. She said how good you had been to her; and at the very time when the poor child needs protection so much, I should be sorry to deprive her of yours."

"I can only thank you heartily, and say how happy I am, sir, that the poor child, not having applied to me, should have sought refuge with you."

Thereupon I wrote the address: "Rue Neuve Saint Augustin; first floor; the folding doors of green velvet. From me-" and I signed: Christian.

I was not known by any other name in the house.

"You will pardon my being so inquisitive, sir," said the Countess; "but when do you intend calling upon her?"

"This evening, Madam."

"Will she be in this afternoon?"

"I am certain she will be at home. You will find her, I have no doubt reading Mademoiselle de Maupin."

"Did you put that book into her hands?"

"Oh no, Madam, she reads any books she likes."

"I have some business in the Rue de la Paix, after which I shall go to see her."

I bowed and escorted the Countess as far as the staircase. I then ran to the window and saw the carriage follow the Rue de Rivoli and turn the corner of the Place Vendome.

I at once took my hat and ran downstairs and was at the Rue Saint Augustin in a moment. I had the key of the passage, so I entered noiselessly the dressing room, and, through an opening made on purpose, I saw Violette sitting in a kind of easy chair, with no other garments than her chemise and half opened dressing gown, with her book on her knees, abstractedly playing with one of her little rosebuds peering out of the masses of her black curls flowing on her breast. Scarcely was I installed at my post of observation than Violette showed signs of being aware that there had been a knock at the door.

The young girl stretched out her arm to ring for the lady's maid: she no doubt suddenly recollected that she had gone out, and, rising, she went slowly and noiselessly to the door.

There was another knock.

"Who is there?" asked Violette.

"I; your friend."

"My friend?"

"Yes; the Countess. I come with M. Christian's consent and am the bearer of a note from him."

"Oh, then," said Violette, who knew the voice and recollected our conversation; "you are welcome." Upon which she opened the door.

The Countess came in and carefully closed the door.

"Are you alone?" she asked.

"Quite alone."

"And your maid?"

"She is at the dressmaker's."

"Ah! so much the better; because as I made sure of finding you here, and wishing to spend a few moments with you, I sent away my carriage. I shall take a cab when I leave you. Will you grant me an hour or two in your company?"

"Yes; with the greatest pleasure."

"Are you pleased to see me?"

"Much pleased."

"You little ungrateful one!"

Meanwhile the Countess took off her veil, bonnet and cloak and appeared in a long dress of black satin, buttoned all the way up with rose coloured buttons. She wore earrings of the same kind of coral.

"I ungrateful?" said Violette. "Why do you call me ungrateful?"

"Why? You went and entrusted yourself to a young man, instead of having recourse to me."

"I did not know your name, nor your address or number. Don't you recollect that you were to come today to see me at: two o'clock at the milliner's shop?"

"I did go there, but the bird had flown. It is true that you did not lose by changing your cage. I congratulate you on the one you occupy now."

"Do you think this one pretty?" asked Violette.

"Delightful! When a painter sets himself to decorating an apartment, he does it with such taste!" Then approaching Violette, she said: "Now, dear little one, I have not even kissed you."

She took her head with both hands and kissed her lips passionately. Violette instinctively drew back to avoid the kiss, but the Countess kept hold of her.

"Do look now," she said, beginning to thee and thou her; "how your charming head is set off by the black satin dress." And she led her to the mirror placed between the two windows. The beautiful fair locks of the Countess fell over Violette's face and mingled with her black hair.

"A! I should have liked to be fair-haired," said Violette.

"Why so?"

"Because I think fair-haired women are much prettier than dark ones."

"Do you really speak the truth, my jewel?"

"Oh yes!" said Violette, looking at the Countess with more curiosity than desire.

"As for me, I am only half a blonde," said the Countess.

"How is that?"

"My eyes and eyebrows are black."

"But they are very pretty!" said Violette innocently.

"Then you think that I am very handsome?"

"Exceedingly handsome!"

"You little flatterer!" said the Countess, putting her arm round Violette's waist and drawing her on her lap.

"But I shall fatigue you."

"Never! How warm it is here, little one."

"But you are buttoned up as if it were winter."

"You are right, I can hardly breathe. If I were certain nobody would come, I should take off my corset."

"Have no fear. Nobody will come."

"There," said the Countess; and in a moment she unbuttoned her dress and took off her corset, keeping on only a long cambric under gown and her satin dress, which she partly buttoned up again.

"And you, do you not feel too warm in your cashmere dress?"

"Oh, no, see how light it is."

It was now Violette's turn to undo the bodice of her gown and appear in her pretty cambric chemise and with her naked feet in velvet slippers. The two globes on her breasts showed admirably under the light texture.

"But do look at the little witch," said the Countess. "She is not yet a woman, and her bosom is larger than mine!"

With this remark she slipped her hand in the opening of Violette's chemise.

"How marvellous," she murmured; "and the nipple is rosy, like a blonde's. Ah, little darling; that is quite the counterpart of the contrast between my fair hair and black eyebrows. Let me kiss this little nipple."

Violette looked about her as if she wished to ask for my leave, though she was not aware of my presence. But the mouth of the Countess was at once glued to her breast, and not only did she kiss the nipple, but she bit it also, gently using her tongue to good purpose the while.

Violette could not refrain from giving expression to the pleasurable sensations which she experienced.

"Ah! see the little imp!" said the Countess. "It is hardly come into the world, and already it seeks pleasures like a grown up woman."

"It is the other one's turn now, for it would be jealous if I did not kiss it too." She took the other nipple which she sucked as she had done the first.

"Oh, Madame, what are you doing?" said Violette.

"Why, I caress you, sweet darling. Did you not see from the first day that I was in love with you?"

"Can one woman be in love with another?" asked Violette, with an innocent look that would have tempted a saint, and, a fortiori, the Countess.

"You little silly," she replied. "That is the only good thing in the world."

Then in a rage with her dress: "You nasty dress! How uncomfortable it is! I will take it off, shall I not?"

"Do as you please, Madame la Comtesse."

"Do not call me so respectfully 'Madame la Comtesse'," she cried, tearing off her dress with such impetuosity that she made the buttons fly.

"But how shall I call you?"

"Call me Odette; that is my nom de guerre."

And her only garment now being the cambric under-gown, she threw herself back on the lounging chair where Violette was reclining, buttoning up her dressing gown to protect herself from the attacks of the Countess.

"Well, what does this mean, you little rebel?" cried the Countess. "Have you by chance taken it into your head to resist?"

"Resist whom?"

"Me, of course."

"Why should I resist you? You do not wish to hurt me, I suppose?"

"No, just the reverse," said the Countess, divesting her of her dressing gown. "No; I wish to give you pleasure, but then you must allow me to do all I please."

"But then... Madame la Comtesse?"

"Odette, you mean. Call me Odette, I tell you!"

"But when you are..."

"Thou! not you!"

"Well; when thou art... Oh! I shall never dare to do so."

"Thou!... Thou! I say," she repeated. "Are we not good friends?"

"Well, yes. That is to say, I am a poor working girl and you are a great lady."

"Well! What should that great lady do to be forgiven for being a Countess, you proud little thing? Behold, I am at your knees. Are you satisfied?"

Indeed, the countess went down on her knees before Violette, who sat in a chair, and gently lifted her chemise in order to gaze upon certain secret charms of which she had caught a glimpse when trying on the drawers. Her eager eyes peered into the arch which her two hands formed in the cambric.

"Oh! what lovely treasures!" she murmured. "How well made! What round thighs! What a soft skin! What marble was it that you were carved out of, dear Hebe? In Paris or Carrara? And this little black dot! Come, let me kiss it!"

She imprinted her lips on it.

"What a nice perfume! Why you little coquette, it is Eau de Portugal!"

"That is Christian's favourite scent."

"Christian? Who's that, I should like to know?"

"Why, he is my lover," said Violette.

"Your lover!... You have a lover?"

"Yes."

"And that lover has had you?"

"Well! yes."

"You are no longer a virgin?"

"No."

"Since when?"

"Since two days ago."

"Oh!!..."

The Countess uttered a cry of rage.

"Oh! the little fool!" she went on, "to think she gave her virginity to a man."

"To whom else could I give it?"

"To me! To me! I would have given you your weight in gold for it. Ah!" said she, in a despairing tone. "I will never forgive you for this."

And she caught up her stays and dress as if about to dress herself again.

"What did your lover do to you? He hurt you cruelly; dare you say he did not; dare you say he gave you pleasure!"

"Oh yes, he did!" cried Violette.

"That is false!"

"Such pleasure as I never could have imagined."

"That is false!"

"I thought I should have become mad with happiness."

"Hold your tongue!"

"What does it matter to you?"

"What! What does it matter to me? Why, it is so much happiness he has robbed me of. I who thought you un-defiled as yet; who wished to initiate you little by little into love's mysteries; I who would have invented for you a new pleasure every day. He polluted you with his coarse caresses! That rough skin, covered with hairs; do you mean to tell me it was pleasant to touch?"

"Ah! Dear Christian has a skin like a woman's!"

"Well, I see I have no chance against him! Good-bye." And mad with rage she put on her corset.

"Are you going away?" asked Violette.

"What can I do here now? Nothing. You have a lover! Oh, I suspected as much directly I saw the warmth with which you took his part against me."

She dressed herself rapidly.

"One more fond illusion flown away!" said she. "Ah! how unhappy to wish to uphold the dignity and pride of our sex. I expected so much pleasure with you, you wicked child! I must weep or my heart will break."

She fell sobbing on a chair. Her tears were so genuine, her grief so intense, that Violette got up without thinking of putting on her dressing gown, and, half naked, went in her turn to kneel before her.

"Come, Madame la Comtesse; do not cry so," said she.

"What? Madame la Comtesse, again!"

"Come, Odette, you are unjust."

"What, 'YOU' again?"

"Thou art unjust."

"How?"

"Could I see that you loved me?"

"You did not see it then, when you called at my house?"

"I suspected nothing. I was so innocent."

"And you are not innocent now?"

"Not quite as much as I was," said Violette, laughing.

The Countess wrung her hands in despair.

"She laughs at my grief!" cried she.

"No, I swear I do not. I swear it!" The Countess shook her head.

"Ah! All is over now! I could forgive, but I shall never forget! But I must not be weak. Adieu! You will never see me more! Adieu."

And the Countess beside herself with grief, like a lover who has just discovered the unfaithfulness of his mistress, opened the door and rushed downstairs.

Violette waited for a moment and listened, thinking she would return; but the angry woman had indeed left for good. Violette closed the door, and turning round, perceived me at the entrance to the dressing room. She uttered a cry of surprise. I burst out laughing, and she threw herself into my arms.

"Ah! how happy I feel now that I was not naughty!" said she.

"Did you find it difficult?"

"Not too much. I must confess, however, that when she kissed my bosom a kind of burning sensation went through my whole frame."

"So that, now, I should not have to use violence."

"Oh, no."

I took her in my arms and seated her in the lounging chair in the same position in which the Countess had placed her.

"You told her it was my favourite scent. Will you let me try it?"

"Ah!" murmured she, after a pause, which was more eloquent than all the speeches in the world. "She told me that you gave me no pleasure!"

"Do you know," said I, "that the dear Countess wore her war dress? Has she not a nom de guerre? She very actively divested herself of her stays and gown. I thought I should see her in still more simple costume."

"You would have been glad of that, you naughty boy!"

"I confess that your two bodies side by side would have formed a charming contrast."

"A thing you never shall see, sir."

"Who knows?"

"She is gone!"

"Nonsense, she will return."

"You think she will return at once?"

"No."

"Did you not see how angry she was?"

44

"I wager that before tomorrow morning she will write to you."

"Must I accept the letter if one should come?"

"Yes; provided you let me see it."

"Oh! of course I shall do nothing without your consent."

"You promise?"

"I give you my word."

"Then I leave you free to act."

At that very moment someone tapped softly at the door, Violette knew at once it was the maid.

My clothes were disarranged, so I ran to the dressing room.

"Open the door," I said.

The maid held a letter in her hand.

"Miss Violette," said she, "the negro who came with the lady has just brought this for you."

"Does he await a reply?"

"No, because he asked me to deliver it to you when you were alone."

"You know Madame Leonie, that these precautions are quite useless, and that I have nothing to conceal from M. Christian."

"Quite so, Miss. In any case, here is the letter."

Violette took it; Leonie left the room and I made my reappearance.

"Well," I said to her, "you see she did not even wait until tomorrow."

"You are truly a good prophet," said Violette, brandishing the letter.

Then she sat on my knee and we began reading the Countess' letter.

CHAPTER 5

"Ungrateful child! Though, when I left you, I swore never to see you again and never to write to you even, my love for you, or rather my folly is, such that I cannot resist. Now mark me, I am rich, a widow, and free. I lived a life of misery with my husband, so I vowed eternal hatred to men, and I kept my vow. If you wish to love me, but mind, only me, I shall willingly forget that you have been sullied by man. You told me that you were not aware that I loved you. My love is such that I take your word for a justification of it-you did 'not know' and I cling to it. Ah! were you only unsullied!... But complete happiness is not to be found in this world. Therefore I am fain to take you such as my bad fortune has ordained.

"Well, if you will love me; if you are willing to forsake him, if you promise never to see him more-I will not say I will give you this or that; but I say: what is mine, shall be yours; we shall live together; my house, my carriage, my servants, shall be your own. We shall never leave one another. You shall be my friend, my sister, my darling child. You will be more than that-you will be my adored mistress! But you must be mine entirely. I am too jealous! Otherwise I should die!

"Give me a prompt reply. I shall await your letter as a condemned one, on death's threshold awaits a reprieve.

ODETTE."

Violette looked at me and we both laughed.
"Well" I said to her; "it is clear she does not mince matters."
"She is mad!"
"Yes. Mad with love for you, that's as plain as a pikestaff. What shall you do?"

46

"Why, I shall not reply."

"No such thing. You must reply."

"What for?"

"Why, you would not like to be responsible for her death?"

"Ah, Monsieur Christian, you wish to see the Countess in a state of nature!"

"But you know very well that she hates men!"

"Yes, but you will make her like them."

"Now, hark you little Violette, if you do not like it..."

"No. Only promise me one thing."

"What's that?"

"You will not make complete love to her."

"What do you mean by complete love?"

"I allow you to use your eyes, your hands, your tongue even! But I keep the other thing for myself."

"I swear it!"

"On what?"

"On our love. And now let us think of her ladyship's letter. The situation which she offers you is not to be despised."

"I leave you? Never! You may dismiss me from your home; you may send me adrift. Since I came to you of my own accord, you have a perfect right to do so. But I would rather die than leave you."

"Then let us say nothing more about it."

"Then we must find some other means."

"I think so too. You must write this."

"What?"

"Take the pen."

"Never mind. The Countess would willingly pay a Louis for each of your misspelt words."

"Then, if I write twenty-five lines, it will cost her twenty-five Louis?"

"Never you mind. Now write away."

"-il write." Violette took the pen and thus wrote from my dictation:

"Madame la Comtesse:

"I fully understand that a life such as you offer me would be happiness; but I have been too hasty, and if my present life is not happiness, I have at least found some tinge of it in the arms of the

47

man I love. I would not leave him for any consideration in the world. He would perhaps be soon reconciled to my loss, for they say that men are changeful; but as for me, I know that I should henceforth live in sorrow.

"I am grieved to give you such a reply. You have been so good to me that I love you with all my heart, and if we were not kept apart by social distinctions, I should wish to be your friend; though I can understand that you would not much care to have for your friend a woman you would have liked for a mistress.

"In any case, whether I see you again or not, I shall ever keep in my remembrance the sensations which I experienced, the kiss that you imprinted on my bosom and the impression of your breath when your mouth touched my body. When I think of that kiss, I close my eyes and sigh-I feel happy.... I ought not to mention this for it looks very much like a confession. But I do not speak now to the beautiful Countess; I speak to my dear Odette!"

and I added, still dictating:

"Your little Violette, who has given away her heart, but keeps her soul for you!"

"No," said Violette, throwing down her pen. "I cannot write that!"

"Why?"

"Because my heart and my soul are yours. Perhaps you do not wish them to be so any longer; but I cannot take them away from you now."

"Ah! my darling!"

I took her in my arms and kissed her again and again.

"Ah!" said I. "I would give all the countesses in the world for one of those fine hairs which stick to my moustache when-"

Violette put her hand on my lips. It was not the first time that I have noticed that, like refined natures, she would allow me to do anything, enjoyed it too, but had an instinctively chaste ear.

I often found this delicate anomaly among women who have inquisitive eyes, a ready mouth, sensual olfactory nerves, and clever hands.

"Well," she asked, "what are you going to do with this letter?"

"I shall send it to the Countess."

"Through the post or by messenger?"

"If you wish to have an answer tonight, send a messenger."

"She will not reply."

"The Countess not reply! Nonsense! She is fairly hooked on now, and cannot withdraw."

"Send it by messenger then. You cannot realize how much all this affair amuses me. I am impatient for an answer."

"I am going to send it. I have company tonight at my house, and shall be here at nine o'clock. Should a letter come, do not reply before I arrive."

"I will not even open it."

"That would really be asking too much of you."

"You can ask anything except asking me to love you no more!"

"Then I shall be here at nine," said I, with a couple of kisses.

"I shall expect you."

I closed her lips with a third kiss and left the room.

At the corner of the Rue Vivienne I met a commission-naire and gave him the letter with the necessary instructions.

I was so impatient to see the answer that at a quarter of nine I made my appearance at the Rue Neuve Saint Augustin.

Violette came to me with a letter in her hand.

"You cannot reproach me with being late," said I, pointing to the clock.

"Is it for me or for the Countess that you made so much haste?" said Violette, laughing.

I took the letter and put it into my pocket.

"Well! What are you doing?"

"That's all right. We have plenty of time to read it; we can open it tomorrow morning."

"Why not before tomorrow morning?"

"So that you may foe sure that I come for you and not for the Countess."

Violette threw her arms round my neck.

"Do I know how to kiss well?" she asked.

"No one could do it better."

"It was you who taught me."

"Just as I taught you that the tongue is not only used for speech."

"But minc has not been used as yet for any other purpose, except the part it takes in kissing."

"The countess will show you that it can be employed in other ways."

"Let us read the letter."

"You wish it?"

"I beg of you."

"Well, wait till nine o'clock."

"Ah! you know," said she, "if you put your hand there, I shall never hear the clock strike."

"I think we had better read the letter at once then."

We were both very eager to be acquainted with the contents of the letter, so I broke the seal and read as follows:

"Dear Little Violette:

"I do not know whether the letter I received from you was penned by you, or whether it was dictated to you, but if it is really yours, truly you are a little imp. On leaving you at three o'clock I vowed I would not write to you. On receiving your letter I vowed again I would never see you more, and I read half of it while protesting that I would not break my vow. But lo! your-style is quite altered in the second part of the letter, you little imp. You now speak of the sensations you experienced. At the very first word the veil which I had thrown upon my recollections is torn aside. I see you lying on the couch. I am now pressing to my lips the rosebud of your breast which meets my mouth half way. I can now hold your letter with one hand only. My eyes are getting dim!

"How foolish I am! I can now do nothing else but murmur your name and repeat: 'Violette, you ungrateful little flower which brought me so much sorrow, such as you are, I long for you.... I must have you.... I love you."

"But no, it is not true I hate you, I will not see you again; and I curse my hand, over which I had no longer any control. I curse the passion which guides it! I take up again the letter which slipped out of my fingers as they clung to the pillow of my couch. I read that line where you recall the sensation of my breath on your form; I see that dark and perfumed spot for which I longed, and on which I was about to imprint my lips, when one single word.... But I do not hear now what you said; I do not remember now; I will not remember; all my memory is in my eyes. Heavens! what beautiful thighs! what a splendid form! How pretty must be all that I could not see!... And now for the second time.... No, I will not. I am mad! for tomorrow I should be ashy pale; I should look ugly! Ah! you pitiless charmer! No; I will not do it! Violette, your mouth... your bosom.... your.... Oh, gracious! When shall I see you again?

Your own,

ODETTE,

"Who is quite ashamed of herself."

"Well" said I, "that is what I call passion, or I am much mistaken. I must make a sketch of you both at the supreme moment."

"Monsieur Christian!..."

"Come, tell me what you will say to her?"

"You know very well that you dictate, and that I have only to hold the pen."

"Then write as follows":

"Dear Odette,

"Christian leaves me at nine o'clock in the morning; I then take my bath. You invited me to take a bath with you. I now propose that you should take one with me, though I cannot guess what pleasure you expect to derive from it.

"I have not the slightest idea of what love between two women may be; you must, in this respect, initiate me into the mystery. I am wholly ignorant, to my shame be it said.

"But with you I am sure I shall soon be proficient, for I love you.

Your, VIOLETTE."

She sealed the letter and called Leonie.

"Give that to a messenger," she said.

"And mind you have it sent this evening," I added.

"Trust to me for that, the letter shall be delivered tonight," replied the maid, and thereupon she left the room.

But she soon returned.

"Miss Violette," said she, "the black servant of Madame la Comtesse inquires whether there is a reply to his mistress' letter. Shall I give him the one you just handed to me?"

"Yes, give it to him without a moment's delay."

Leonie left the room, this time for good.

"Well, she was in a great hurry, this charming Countess," I said.

"Do what you like, I leave you free to follow your own inclination."

"Very well. Meanwhile I shall make you as happy as I can."

CHAPTER 6

The next day, at five minutes to nine, Violette was in a bath perfumed with verbena, and I in a cupboard in a corner of the room, whence I could see and hear everything. All traces of my presence had disappeared, and the sheets had been changed and sprinkled with eau-de-Cologne.

At exactly nine o'clock a carriage stopped at the door.

A moment later, the Countess was ushered in by Leonie, who left and closed the door, which was instantly bolted by the Countess.

The bathroom was lighted up by a lamp in a rose-coloured vase of Bohemian glass, which shed a soft and discreet light.

"Violette! Violette" cried the Countess, "where art thou?"

"Here, in the dressing room," replied the young girl.

The Countess sprang across the room in three strides, and stopped at the door.

Violette nearly stood up in the bath, showing her Nerean-like form, with arms outstretched.

"Oh! my darling!" cried the Countess, throwing her self into her arms.

She was clad in a long blouse of black velvet, fastened at the neck by a large diamond and held at the waist by a Russian belt woven with gold, silver and cherry-coloured silk.

She began by pulling off her boots and her rose-coloured dress, unfastened her belt and divested herself of her blouse.

Under the black velvet blouse she wore a cambric peignoir, edged with Valenciennes round the neck and cuffs.

She then slipped off the peignoir and appeared in a nude state.

The Countess was a truly splendid woman; the type of Diana the huntress. Her chest was more fully developed than her breasts; her waist was as pliant as the stem, of a tree that waves in the breeze; the parts below were perfection, and lower still might be seen a mass of luxuriant and reddish hair, which resembled flames shooting out of a crater.

She went to the bath and wished to enter it.

But Violette stopped her.

"Ah! Let me feast my eyes upon your charms," said she. "You are so beautiful!"

"Do you really think so, sweet darling?"

"Oh, yes, I do."

"Look on, then, look on! that I may feel the burning sensation of your eyes upon me. See, all this is yours! See! My eyes, my mouth, my bosom..."

"And this pretty bouquet also?" asked Violette.

"Oh yes! That especially!"

"What a beautiful colour!" said the young girl. "Why is it not the same as that of your chevelure?"

"Why should not my chevelure be of the same colour? Why am I a woman not fond of men? Because I am a compound of contrasts. Come, sweet love, make room for me, that I may feel my heart beat against thine."

The bath was long and there was room for both. The Countess stepped in and sat beside Violette.

The water, as transparent as crystal, allowed me to see everything.

The Countess entwined herself with snake-like movements round Violette; she passed her head under her arm, took a little bite there, and put her lips on Violette's mouth.

"Ah!" she said, "at last you are mine, you naughty child, and now I shall be revenged for all the tortures I endured for your sake.

"Approach your mouth, your lips, your tongue. When I think that it was a man who first gave you a kiss of that kind; who taught you to return it, I am half inclined to strangle you!"

And like a serpent shooting its head forward, the Countess darted kiss upon kiss, while her hand fondled Violette's bosom:

"Oh, darling breasts, my sweet ones!" murmured the Countess. "It was through you that I lost my head; it is you who have made me mad with passion!"

And she caressed them, half closing her eyes, throwing her head back, and breathing hard.

"But do speak to me, rapture of my soul!" she said.

"Odette, dear Odette!" murmured Violette.

"How she does say that, the little frigid thing. She says it as she would say 'Good morning!' Are you not afraid that your own Christian would hear you? Wait, wait, and we shall add a sharp to the key to make the note half a tone higher." And her hand slipped from the bosom to the hips and thence lower still; but at that stage it stopped as if hesitating.

"Do you feel my heart throbbing against your breast? Ah! If it could kiss your own as my mouth presses your lips!... if it could!... Do you feel anything?"

"Yes," murmured Violette, who began to feel the forerunner of pleasure. "Yes! Your finger, is it not?"

"You are so young, so little experienced, that I can hardly find the darling little love nipple which gives the flower of life to all nature! Ah, now! Here it is!..."

"How soft your finger is! What a gentle and delightful touch."

"Shall I do it faster, more vigorously?"

"No, no! It is quite nice as it is."

"But your own hands; where are they?"

"I told you that I knew nothing and that you would have to teach me."

"What? Even teach you how to have a sensation?"

"Oh, no! That will come... will come of its own accord. Odette!... Dear Odette!... Odette!..."

The Countess caught up the remainder of the sigh in a kiss.

"That's right," said she. "It is not enough to be able to speak a language; you must use the right accent, too."

"I am a willing pupil," said Violette, "I ask for nothing better than to learn."

"Then let us leave the bath. I cannot put my head under water; and I have to add something in speech to my demonstration."

"Yes," said Violette, "there is a fire and warm towels."

"Come," said the Countess, "I will wipe your body dry."

She came out dripping with the glistening drips of water, beautiful as Thetas, proud like her. She thought she had vanquished her rival-that is, your humble servant-and looked quite triumphant.

Violette. borne in her arms, cast a glance towards me as if to say: "All that I am doing is in obedience to your orders."

All the curtains were drawn and the room was lighted up only by the glitter of the fire.

Both came to the fireplace shivering. But the Countess thought only of Violette. I could hear her, while plying the towels, praise the parts of the form on which her hand rested in turn. Each received its share of caresses, of eulogy. The neck, arms, back, shoulders, breasts-all came, so to speak, in chronological order. As for herself, the heat of her person sufficed to dry her skin. Violette remained passive under the caresses of the Countess.

Now and then the Countess would upbraid her.

"But you do not think my breasts are beautiful? I suppose so, since you will not kiss them. Do you not find my hair soft enough for your pretty fingers? I must tell you that I am all afire, and that presently you must in your turn, return all the pleasure I give you."

"But, dear Odette," replied Violette, "you know very well that I am a little ignoramus."

"Yes; but you said also you were willing to learn. Well, I will teach you."

I saw them pass before me in a state of perfect nudity.

The Countess carried Violette to the bed and laid her across it, knelt on the black bearskin, parted her thighs and gazed longingly on that charming sanctuary of love; then suddenly, with nostrils dilated, her lips curled up, and with teeth like those of a panther eager for its prey, she pressed her lips to it.

This mode of caressing is generally a cause of triumph for a woman who seeks to defeat a male rival. She must, by dint of skill and agility, leave no cause for regret to the mistress with whom she plays a part which is not natural to her.

It seems that, when promising rapturous pleasures to Violette, the Countess had not made an empty boast. I felt rather jealous when I saw my dear little mistress roll about, writhe and pant, and almost faint under the greedy mouth which seemed to wish to inhale even her very soul.

It is true that, for a painter, the sight was most interesting and amply compensated me for the little fit of jealousy to which I humbly confess I gave way.

The Countess on her knees, and well settled on her heels, followed with her body, all the movements of Violette's body and her beauteous form writhed about so that I could have sworn she lost nothing in being the active instrument, and that perhaps she even gained something by it.

At last both performers exhausted by their efforts, were fain to lie side by side and take a rest.

"Ah!" murmured the Countess, "you must repay part of your debt to me." And with these words she drew Violette close to her, took her hand, and placed it on that tawny part of her person which formed such a contrast to her blonde hair and black eyebrows.

But Violette had her instructions and acted up to them marvellously. No doubt the Countess had occasion to find fault with her, for I heard her whisper: "That is not the right spot, your finger is too high... There, there; now it is too low. Do you not feel something there?

Well that is where you must act. It is this tickling which brings pleasure. Ah! you are doing it on purpose, you naughty little thing!"

"I assure you I am not," replied Violette. "I am doing my best to please you."

"When you have hit the right place why do you withdraw your finger? There you are at it again!"

"My finger slips."

"Oh! You have set me all afire, and you do nothing to extinguish the flames!"

"Listen, my handsome lover," said Violette, "let us try something else."

"What?"

"Lie down on the bed with your head towards the mirror, and I will caress you with my mouth.

"I will do all you wish."

The Countess lay at full length, with eyes to the ceiling, her thighs well parted and her body curved by the rotundity of the bed.

This was the moment agreed upon, and I crawled out of the dressing room.

"Am I in a convenient posture?" inquired Odette, with a final motion of her back.

"Yes, I think you are," replied Violette.

"There now; you can begin."

I followed to the letter the instructions that were given to my little friend.

"Is that the right place?" asked Violette.

"Yes. And now... your mouth... And mind, if you do not give me pleasure, I shall strangle you."

I applied my mouth to the spot and had no trouble in finding the thing which Violette pretended not to have found. It was all the easier, because I noticed that in the case of the Countess it was longer than usual. It seemed to be the nipple of a virgin's breast excited by a lover's lips. I seized it in my mouth, and rolled it gently between my lips.

The Countess heaved a voluptuous sigh.

"Oh!" said she, "that is just the thing; and I think that if you keep on like that... I think... I think you will no longer be in my debt."

I went on as she bid Violette, but drew the latter to me and pointed out to her the part she was to take in the trio.

But with me Violette was not clumsy as with Odette. Divining the thousand caprices of love's pleasures, she placed her mouth where I had put her hand, and I found that she was doing to me the very counterpart of what I did to the Countess, save that there was a difference in the shape of the objects performed upon.

The Countess seemed to experience the most voluptuous pleasures.

"Oh! really," said she, "it is just as I like it. Ah! you little story teller, you said I must teach you; but you are too clever.... not so fast!... I wish it lasted forever... forever! Oh! your tongue...."

Had I been able to speak I would have paid just the same compliments to Violette. The passionate child had certainly the instinct of all the artifices of love.

I own I derived considerable pleasure from the caresses which I lavished upon the Countess. Never had I pressed my lips upon a sweeter peach. In this woman of twenty-eight all was firm and youthful as in a girl of eighteen. It was easy to perceive that the brutality of man had exercised itself there only to open a way for more delicate caresses.

The Countess gave expression to her wonder and admiration.

"Oh!" said she, "how strange, I never had such pleasure before. Oh! I will not let you go on unless you promise to commence again. The impression of your lips and your tongue is so sweet; I cannot keep it back any longer! It is coming! I feel it! I feel it! No! It cannot be Violette who gives me so much pleasure; it is impossible!"

Violette did not at all feel inclined to reply.

"Violette, tell me, is it you! Oh, no! That is impossible. You are too clever for a woman. A woman could never do this!"

The Countess tried to raise herself up, but with my hands firmly pressed to her breasts I kept her down. Besides the supreme sensation was nigh; I was quite aware of that. So I redoubled my efforts, and my moustache began to play its part in the tickling. The Countess writhed and almost shrieked; then I felt the climax had come; my lips gave the finishing touch, and the amorous spasm shook the whole frame of the Countess.

My excitement had also reached the highest pitch, and I gave way to it at the very same moment.

Violette was lying half dead at my feet.

I had not sufficient strength left to prevent the Countess from rising from the bed.

At a single glance she realized how matters stood, and, springing up, she cried out with anger.

"Well, dear Violette," said I, "I have done my best to quarrel with the Countess. You must now be the peacemaker."

Thereupon I retreated to the dressing room.

Then a stormy scene took place. I heard cries, reproaches, and finally sighs, and I looked out, and saw Violette who had taken my place near the Countess, doing her best to make my peace with her.

"Ah!" said the Countess, when Violette had concluded her speech. "I must say that this is good; but just now it was exquisite!"

And she gave me her hand. So we were friends again.

CHAPTER 7

In the agreement drawn up between the belligerents it was enacted:

First, that Violette should remain my sole property.

Second, that I should lend her occasionally to the Countess, but always in my presence.

Thirdly, that I should play with the Countess the part of a woman just as much as I pleased, but never that of a man.

The agreement was drawn up in triple copies and duly signed by the contracting parties. A clause was added by which it was agreed that in case Violette and the Countess failed to fulfil any of the conditions of the said agreement, I should thereby be entitled for a space of time not exceeding the duration of their crim con., to rights on the Countess similar to those I enjoyed over Violette.

Violette feared at first that my love for her would be diminished in consequence of the kind of association agreed upon. I might have entertained a similar fear, but this new mode of life, far from having the expected result, only fanned the fire of our love into fiercer flames by enhancing its pleasures.

As we strictly adhered to the various clauses of our agreement, there could be no jealousy on either side.

But such was not the case with the Countess. Every time I acted the part of a lover with Violette, the young girl was compelled to transmit my caresses, in another form to the Countess.

As I had not bound myself with respect to the Countess, in the same way that she was bound to me-that is, that she was never to touch Violette except in my presence-I could enjoy my dear little mistress as often as I liked, and I never found my happiness incomplete because of the absence of the Countess. I must own that, as an artist, I derived much benefit from this mode of living. Often, in the midst of our passionate embraces, I would jump off the bed, seize my album and pencil, and, far from seeking to impede the fiery ardour of my two models, I excited it to the utmost, so as to produce lascivious and novel combinations which exhibited their beauteous forms in new and delightful outlines.

But all this did not make me forget Violette's plans for the future, and her natural bent for a theatrical career.

I made her learn Racine's Iphigenie, Moliere's La Fausse Agnes, and Hugo's Marion Delorme, and I perceived that she had great talent for acting light comedy.

The countess had been educated at the Convent des Oiseaux, and had there frequently taken a part in various comedies at holiday times, as is customary at ladies' educational establishments. Her tall figure and almost masculine voice allowed her to impart to her stage play and delivery a certain masterly colour.

So I derived much pleasure from seeing them act together, when, draped in the real Greek robes which leave certain parts of the body in a nude state, they gave themselves up to the sweet and yet powerful accents of passion which distinguish Racine's masterpiece.

When I had made sure of her inborn vocation, and taken the advice of one of my friends, a well-known playwright, I asked him for a letter of recommendation to a certain professor of the dramatic art.

He gave it to me with a smile, saying that I should warn Violette of the amorous disposition of M.X.

I took Violette to M.X. and handed the letter to him. We made her act three different parts in succession, and this gentleman came also to the conclusion that she was most fitted for light comedy.

He gave her the part of Cherubin to learn. Everything went well for the first three weeks, but after, Violette one evening threw herself on my neck, and shaking her head, said to me:

"Christian, I cannot go any more to M.X."

I asked her the reason.

My friend's suppositions had been realized. During the first four or five lessons the master showed his pupils nothing but truly brotherly regard, but once, under pretence of teaching her how to match the stage play with the delivery, he put his hands upon her person and took liberties with her. Violette was obliged to shrink from his touch, which looked more like that of a lover than that of a teacher.

Violette settled with him for the price of her lessons, and never returned to his place.

It thus became necessary to provide her with another professor.

The new one acted very nearly in the same manner as the first.

One day, at the hour appointed for the lesson, she did not find him in his study, but saw on his desk an open book instead of the Moliere which usually served for her part.

It was an obscene book with engravings to match the text. Instinctively she glanced at it. The title was Philosophic Therese.

This title did not enlighten her, but the first engraving she came upon was unmistakable.

This book might have been left there by chance. Violette declared such was not the case, and that she would not go to that professor again.

Violette was as passionate as could be, but she did not like indecencies. During the three years she lived with me, we went through the entire scale of Love's ardent caresses, but never did a coarse word issue from her lips.

We settled accounts with this new professor, and then began pondering as to the means of protecting her against such attempts.

I hit upon the plan of procuring for her a lady teacher. I sought the advice of one of my friends, a celebrated actress. She was intimate with a very clever young lady who had achieved success at the Odeon and Porte Saint Martin. Her name was Florence. Unfortunately this was falling out of the frying pan into the fire, as Florence had the reputation of being one of the most active tribades in Paris.

She never would be married and never had a lover, as far as people knew.

The Countess, Violette and myself held a council. I did not wish to widen the circle of my acquaintances, being fully aware of the drawbacks of a life shared in a thousand ways. Nevertheless I was bent upon developing to its full extent the artistic talent of my dear little mistress.

I pondered a while, and had a conversation with the Countess. I perceived, from the expression of her bright eyes, that the subject of our discussion moved her strongly. Thereupon I quickly persuaded her to introduce herself to the great actress as an admirer of her talents, and to represent Violette as a young girl in whom she took the utmost interest, but at the same time to show a tinge of jealousy sufficiently marked to render Florence cautious. At the very time the actress had just created a part in which she was enabled to give expression to the peculiar passion which she had received from nature. The Countess, who felt much inclination for the part she was about to undertake, took a monthly subscription for a private box in Florence's theatre.

The Countess had assumed masculine garb. She went to her box and raising the green screen, remained visible only to the actress.

It goes without saying that she was exquisite in her fancy dress, consisting of a black velvet frock coat lined with satin, pale green trousers, a buff waistcoat and cherry coloured necktie. Small black moustaches, which matched the eyebrows, aided in making her pass for a young dandy of eighteen.

An expensive bouquet, from the most fashionable florist, lay on a chair near her, and at a convenient moment she threw it at Florence's feet.

An actress to whom bouquets worth thirty or forty francs are thrown four night in succession cannot fail to condescend to glance at the box whence they came.

Florence did glance and saw in the box a charming youth who looked like a collegian. She thought him handsome and amusing and said to herself, "What a pity he is not a woman!"

The next night and following nights the same enthusiasm was displayed by the young man, and the same regret secretly expressed by the actress.

On the fifth night a note was affixed to the bouquet.

Florence saw it but her indifference for our sex caused her to lay it aside. When at home she suddenly thought of it.

She had just partaken of a rather cheerless supper, and was dreaming by the fireplace. She called her maid.

"Mariette," said she, "there was a note in tonight's bouquet. Give it to me."

Mariette brought it in on a china dish.

Florence opened and perused it. At the first line she felt much interested. It was penned in this style:

"Indeed, charming Florence, it is with brow flushed with shame that I write to you, but expect that I shall add, like a madman. Have compassion on me, for I am obliged to confess that I am not what I appear to be, and I must add, I love you like a madwoman!"

"Now rail at me! despise me; spurn me away-all will be sweet to me, even insults, coming from you!

ODETTE."

At the words "I love you like a madwoman" Florence uttered a cry.

Then, as she had no secrets from her maid:

"Mariette! Mariette!" she cried, quite elated. "It is a woman!"

"I suspected as much," replied the maid.

"You foolish, girl, why did you not tell me?"

"I was afraid of being mistaken."

"Ah!" murmured Florence, "how pretty she must be!"

Then after a pause of a few seconds, she asked in a languid voice:

"Where are the bouquets?"

"Madame knows well that, thinking they came from a man, she ordered them thrown away."

"But tonight's bouquet."

"It is still here."

"Give it to me."

Mariette handed it to her.

Florence took it and looked at it with a pleased smile.

"Do you not think it splendid?"

"Not more so than the others."

"Do you not think so?"

"Madame has not even looked at them."

"Ah!" said Florence, laughing. "I shall not be so ungrateful in the case of this one. Help me to undress, Mariette."

"Madame will not keep it in her room, I hope."

"Why not?"

"Because there is a magnolia, some lilac and other strongly scented flowers, which may give you a headache."

"There is no danger of that."

"I beseech Madame to let me take the bouquet away."

"No such thing."

"If Madame wishes to be asphyxiated, she is free to do so, of course."

"If one could be asphyxiated with flowers, don't you think it would be better to die thus at once, instead of lingering on for three or four years with consumption, as my fate will probably be?"

Florence had a short fit of dry cough.

"Should Madame die in three or four years," said Mariette, whilst undressing her mistress, "it will be because Madame wished it."

"How do you make that out?"

"I heard what the doctor said to Madame yesterday."

"What! You heard it?"

"Yes!"

"Then you were listening!"

"No. I was in the dressing room.... One hears sometimes without trying to."

"Well, what did he say?"

"He said it would be better for you to have three or four lovers than to do what you do when you are alone!"

Florence pouted as if in disgust.

"I do not like men!" said she, inhaling the perfume of the bouquet.

"Will Madame sit down while I pull off her stockings?" asked Mariette.

Florence sat down without replying, her face almost hidden in the flowers.

She allowed Mariette to take off her boots and wash her feet with perfumed water.

"What scent will Madame have in her bidet?"

"The same. That which poor Denise liked so much. Do you know that I have now been faithful to her for six months?"

"Yes; at the expense of your health."

"Oh! I think of her when I do that... and when the pleasure comes... murmur, 'Denise!... Denise!'..."

"Will you say Denise again tonight?"

"Hush!" said Florence smiling and putting a finger on her lips.

"Does Madame require anything else?"

"No!"

"If Madame is unwell tomorrow, she will not say it is my fault?"

"If tomorrow I am unwell I will not hold you responsible Mariette, I promise you. Good night, Marietta."

"Good night, Madame."

And she made her exit grumbling the while like a spoiled maid, or worse still, like a maid in possession of all her mistress' secrets.

When she was alone in front of her cheval glass, Florence listened till she no longer heard the retreating footsteps of her maid, then she went barefooted and on tiptoe to fasten the bolt of her bedroom door. She then returned to the looking glass, read again the note of the Countess, kissed it, and laid it on the dressing table within easy reach, unfastened the bouquet, and, undoing the ribbon knot of her chemise, she rested her lips on her body and allowed the chemise to slip to the floor.

Florence was a magnificent brunette, with large blue eyes always encircled with a dark tinge. Her long hair reached down to her knees and half covered a form rather thin and spare, but of magnificent proportions in spite of her state of emaciation.

Mariette's words have given us the explanation of this emaciation. But she could not have accounted, deep as she was in her mistress' confidence, for the abundance of hair which adorned the whole front part of Florence's body.

This curious ornament reached up to the breasts, where it slipped up like the point of a lance. Then it ran downwards in a thin line which joined the mass which covered all the lower part of the abdomen, disappeared between the thighs and reappeared slightly at the lower part of the back.

Florence was very proud of this ornament, which seemed to make of her a compound of both sexes. She tended and perfumed it with jealous care. But what was most remarkable was the fact that her brown but splendid skin did not bear anywhere else the slightest trace of capillary vegetation.

She began by surveying herself with extreme satisfaction, smiling at her own image, then with a soft brush she smoothed down all the charming fur. She then selected the most beautiful flowers in the bouquet and formed them into a crown, which she placed on her head; sprinkled her whole body with tuberoses and jonquils; turned the mount of Venus into a rose garden connected to her breasts by garlands of Parma violets, and thus, covered with flowers, intoxicated with their strong perfumes, she languidly reclined on a long easy chair placed before her cheval glass, so as to be able to survey her whole form. At last, with half closed eyes, her head thrown back, with quivering nostrils, lips curled up, one hand on one of her round breasts, and the other slipping down gradually, as if moved irresistibly to the altar where, as a selfish solitary priestess, she was about to consummate the sacrifice, her finger slowly disappeared among the roses. Nervous motions began to agitate this beautiful statue of pleasure; these involuntary motions were soon followed by unintelligible words, suppressed sighs, then deeper sighs, in the midst of which was muttered no longer the name of Denise, but the no less sweet name of "Odette".

CHAPTER 8

On entering her mistress' room next morning, Mariette cast an investigating glance on all sides. She saw the easy chair before the cheval glass, the carpet is sprinkled with flowers, Florence lying quite exhausted in bed and awaiting her bath.

Mariette shook her head and said:

"Oh! Madame! Madame!"

"Well, what next?" asked Florence opening her eyes.

"When I think that the handsomest gentlemen and the prettiest women in Paris would like to be your slaves!"

"Do I not deserve it?" asked the actress.

"Oh, Madame! I do not mean that. Just the reverse."

"Well, you see, I can very well do without them."

"Madame will not be amended. But really, in her place, were it only out of self-respect, I should have a lover."

"But I cannot bear men. Do you like them, Mariette?"

"Do I like men? No, I do not. But I should certainly like one man."

"Men only care for us from selfish motives-to exhibit us if we are pretty, to show themselves in our company if we are clever. No! If I gave myself up to a man, he would be such a superior being that I should admire, if not love him.

"Alas! my poor girl, I lost my mother before I knew her; my father was a mathematician, who taught me to believe in nothing but straight lines, squares and circles He used to call God the 'Supreme Unity', he called the universe 'the great whole', and death, 'the great problem'.

"He departed this life when I was unable to care for myself, leaving me penniless and devoid of any illusions. I became an actress, and now of what use is my art to me? To despise the work which I act; to find naught but historical heresies in dramas.

"Of what use to me are my intellectual powers? To find in dramas of the heart the shortcomings of sentiment; to shrug my shoulders at the conceit of the authors who read their productions to me. The major part of my success I reproach myself with as I would a bad action, or an encouragement of bad taste. At first I wished to speak on the stage as one speaks in everyday life-I produced no effect. I ranted when speaking-then I gained applause. At first I composed my own parts rationally, poetically, in masterly touches-they said: 'Good; very good'. I then overdid the part and showed the whites of my eyes; I shouted, I screamed-and there were thunders of applause in the house. The men who pay me compliments do not praise my merits, but my faults; and women do not understand my notions of beauty.

"A compliment which misses its mark hurts one as much as any criticism which does hit the mark. But, thank heaven, I make enough money not to need the favours of anybody.

I had rather die than owe anything to a man and have to say to him: 'Here is my body, repay yourself with it!' No, I had rather die!

"I can only bear women because I domineer over them; because I am their master, their lord, their spouse. But they are wayward, wilful and devoid of intellect. With a few exceptions, they are inferior beings, created for submission. I see no merit in subduing a woman. And then she will complain of being tyrannized, and will deceive you.

"No, no! Look you, Mariette, the ideal of domination is to be one's own mistress-to give nobody the right to say: 'You shall obey me.' Nobody has this right over me. I am twenty-two; am a virgin, like Herminice, like Clorinda, like Bradamante, and if ever I get tired of my virginity, I shall sacrifice it to myself. I shall have both the pain and the pleasure. I will not allow a man to be able to say: 'I possessed that woman.' "

"It is Madame's taste, there is nothing to be said."

"It is not my taste, Mariette. It is the outcome of my Philosophy."

"As for me," rejoined Mariette, "I know I should feel much humiliation in dying a virgin."

"That misfortune will certainly not be yours. Come and dress me, Mariette."

Florence left her bed languidly and sat in the easy chair in front of the cheval glass.

Florence, as we said before, was not exactly a pretty woman, but she had most expressive features. She had never loved except in imagination, but could render excellently the utmost violence of passion. Her peculiar talent was one rarely met with, such as that of Dorval or of Malibran.

She took her bath, breakfasted on a cup of chocolate, glanced over her part, read the Countess' letter a dozen times, grew excited over it, dined on some consommé, a couple of stewed truffles and four crawfish a la Bordelaise.

Then she went to the theatre in a state of great excitement.

The handsome young man (or rather the Countess) was in his box, and had a large bouquet on a chair close by.

At the fourth act in the course of a pathetic scene, the Countess threw the bouquet.

Florence picked it up, looked for the note inside, and read it without taking time to return to her box.

The note ran thus:

"Have I obtained your pardon? My impatience is such that I have come in person to seek for an answer. If you have forgiven me, place one of the flowers of my bouquet in your hair. In this case I shall be the most tender of lovers, the most happy of women; and I shall wait for you at the stage door with my carriage, for I hope that instead of going home sadly alone, you will do me the pleasure of supping at my house.

ODETTE."

Florence, without a moment's reflection, plucked a red camellia from the bouquet, put it in her hair, and returned to the stage.

Odette almost threw herself out of the box to applaud, and Florence managed to kiss her hand to her.

Half an hour later, the Countess' carriage, with drawn blinds, was stationed in the rue de Bondy.

Florence hastily got rid of her rouge and stage ornaments, put on a Caucasian dressing gown, and rushed out of the theatre.

The black groom opened the door of the carriage and resumed his place on the box, the coachman put his horses to a rapid trot.

The Countess took Florence in her arms. But the reader is already acquainted with the latter's views concerning her own dignity. Instead of accepting the place which the Countess had provided for her in her arms and on her knees, she seized the Countess in her vigorous grasp, lifted her like a child, and with one movement of her strong arm, like a wrestler who lays low his adversary, she placed Odette across her knees, pressing her lips to hers, put her tongue in her mouth, and her hand between her thighs.

"Surrender, my handsome cavalier, rescue or no rescue!" said Florence, laughing.

"I surrender!" said the Countess, "and I only ask one thing. I do not wish to be rescued, I wish to succumb and die by your hand."

"Then die!" said Florence, with a kind of fury.

Indeed, five minutes later, the Countess, almost in a swoon murmured:

"Oh, dear Florence, how sweet it is to expire in your arms! I die... I die... I die...."

She heaved the last sigh just as the carriage stopped at No...

The two women went up leaning on one another and quite panting with their exertions.

The Countess had the key of her apartments. She opened the door and closed it after them. They crossed the ante-chamber, which was lighted up by a Chinese lantern. Thence they entered the bedroom, which received the light from a lamp of rose-coloured Bohemian glass, and at last the Countess opened the door of a dining room, with a table ready served.

"Dear love," said she "by your leave we will be our own attendants. I should be glad to keep on my gentleman's attire in order to wait upon you, but it would be inconvenient. I will therefore lay aside that horrid masculine dress, and appear in my war harness. Here is the dressing room. I believe it has every convenience, and that you will find all that is necessary."

We have already been introduced to the dressing room of the Countess. It was the very same to which she had taken Violette. A slab of white marble bore bottles of the finest scents from Dubues, Laboullee and Guerlain.

Five minutes after, Odette joined her friend there.

She was nude; at least very nearly so, for she had kept on her rose-coloured silk stockings, blue velvet garters, and slippers of the same material and colour.

It goes without saying that the whole place was heated by a well-regulated warming apparatus.

"You must excuse my dress," said the Countess, laughingly, "but I wish to make a toilette which you rendered necessary, and ask you what scent you prefer."

"Can I make my own choice?" said Florence.

"Please yourself," replied the Countess.

"Well, I perceive there a bottle of eau-de-Cologne. What say you?"

That is not my business," said the Countess. "Let your choice be guided by your own taste."

Florence poured out the contents of an immense water bottle into a charming bidet of Sevres porcelain, mixed a fourth part of the bottle of eau-de-Cologne with it, and proceeded to the Countess' toilette.

"Well," asked the latter, laughing, "what are you doing?"

"I am looking at you, my beautiful mistress, and I admire you!"

"So much the better for you, since I am yours, all in all."

"What marvellous hair! What teeth! What a neck! Oh, let me kiss those pretty nipples. You will think I am hideous, I am sure. I shall never dare to undress in your presence. What a satin-like skin! I shall look like a Negress! And all this beautiful fiery-coloured hair! How marvellous! I shall look like a sweep in comparison."

"You are joking; but do not make me wait. If my hair is the colour of fire, it is because the house is on fire! Now, you must put it out."

The Countess bent forward and her lips met those of Florence, whom she clasped in her arms, then, suddenly rising and resting both hands on her shoulders, she brought her streaming and perfumed body on a level with her lips.

Florence at once pressed her lips to that second mouth, more perfumed still than the other, and which presented itself so unexpectedly; then advancing on her knees while the Countess walked backwards, she pushed the latter to a couch where she fell back, like one of the gladiators of old, with all the gracefulness required in such circumstances.

However little the Countess was used to playing a passive part in encounters of this description, she quickly understood that the dark complexioned and thin woman was endowed with a power of manhood superior to that which she herself possessed. She surrendered in this instance with the same readiness as before, and as the new agent of pleasure was more active and more complicated than its predecessor, she acknowledged its superiority by motions of her body which could not possibly leave Florence in doubt as to the intensity of the pleasurable sensations which she gave the Countess.

For a few seconds the two beautiful women remained motionless. Everybody knows that, in this peculiar mode of procuring Love's pleasures, the sensations of both giver and recipient are alike.

Florence was the first to recover from her trance. She remained for some few seconds on her knees before the Countess, and her eyes, her countenance, her smile, her arms, which in her exhaustion, hung motionless by her sides, all seemed to bear witness to her delight.

Wholly insensible to beauty in man, because she was almost a man herself, Florence worshipped beauty in women; however, she now felt a little uneasy fearing that her type of beauty might not be altogether to the taste of the Countess, a circumstance which the proud girl would have deemed very humiliating.

Thus, when she had recovered, and when the Countess began to disrobe her, Florence set herself to tremble in all her limbs, like a virgin whose unsullied body is about to be defiled by eyes other than her mother's.

But the Countess was impatient. The delightful emanations from Florence's body got into her head and seemed to intoxicate her.

"Come!" she said with a feverish impatience: "Art thou not a woman? Art thou a flower? So be it; then, instead of drinking I shall inhale. Oh! the beautiful, curious thing!" she exclaimed, when she saw Florence's naked body. "Why, that is like silk, like perfumed silk! What is the meaning of it?"

Thereupon the Countess began covering with kisses the charming ornament, which, as we said before, rose to a point as far as the breasts, getting thinner on the stomach and wider lower down, and on which when leaving her box, Florence had scattered a whole bouquet of newly gathered violets.

"Come!" said the astonished Countess; "I confess I am vanquished. Not only are you far more handsome than I am, but you are much prettier!"

Then she led her to the dining room. Both naked, they entered the palace of mirrors, where a thousand crystals reflected at once their beautiful forms and the lights of the chandeliers and lustre's.

They looked at one another for some little time, their arms encircling each other's waists; each proud of her own beauty and that of her companion; then they took two white haicks, one with gold stripes, the other ornamented with silver, as transparent as woven air, and they sat down to supper. All the dishes were most dainty. The iced champagne sparkled in muslin-like decanters, and they began to sip the exhilarating beverage from the same glass, and often from each other's lips.

CHAPTER 9

At first they were attentive to one another as lovers would be together, helping one another to small dainties and titbits, intermixed with burning kisses on the arms, shoulders and lips. Then, after supper, they rose, letting their haicks fall to the floor, the Countess like the goddess Pomona, bearing away some fruit in a basket of golden filigree, and Florence holding in her hand a cup brimming over with sparkling champagne.

They approached the bed with arms encircling each other's waists. Then they looked at one another, as if to say: "Who is going to begin?"

"Ah!" said the Countess, "I think I must begin."

No doubt Florence was satisfied with the reply, for she pressed her lips to those of the Countess, imprinting a burning kiss on her mouth, and she lay on the bed in a posture full of abandon.

The Countess gazed for a moment on the strange form, in which were combined the virility of the man and the gracefulness of woman. She took from her hair the golden comb studded with diamonds, and laid it as a crown on the charming representative of the mysterious Isis, who, foremost of all goddesses, was worshiped under the name of Saunia.

The gold and diamonds sparkled in the black fur, and the comb almost disappeared in it, without reaching however to the aperture which the jealous Countess would have wished to encompass.

Then she went on her knees, and as the magnificent ornament which she had just added to the shrine did not hinder her from paying her respects to it, she gently laid Florence's thighs on her two shoulders, and drew aside the thick fur which closed the entrance to the grotto disclosed to her view, like a casket of black velvet lined with rose-coloured satin.

At this unexpected sight the Countess gave an exclamation of pleasure, and at once began to apply her tongue to the pretty sanctuary; but, to her great astonishment, she perceived that the passage, which she thought free, was closed up. She rose quickly and looking eagerly at Florence, said:

"What does that mean?"

"Why, dear Odette," said Florence laughing, "it means that I am a virgin, or if you prefer it, that I still have my maidenhead."

"Is there any difference?"

"Certainly, my dear. The virgin is a girl that never was touched by anybody; the innocent one who knows nothing of love's pleasures. But she of the maidenhead is the one who in spite of her own private practices, or her intercourse with others, has been able to keep whole the membrane of the Hymen."

"Ah! then I have found a girl whom man never sullied! Oh! my beautiful Florence, I can hardly believe it."

"You can ascertain for yourself," said Florence; "the more so as I have to reproach you with stopping short when I was just about to feel the approach of pleasure. Begin again, my beloved Odette, and should there be any further occasion for astonishment, wait till you have done before you express it."

"One word more?"

"Certainly."

"Then you have still your maidenhead, but you are no longer a virgin?"

"No, indeed I am not."

"Are men responsible for your being no longer a virgin?"

"Not for the world. The gaze of man never rested on my form; never did man touch me."

"Ah!" cried Odette, "that is all I wished to know," and she threw herself on Florence, and applied her lips to the sanctuary.

Florence gave a little shriek. She felt, perhaps too acutely the impression of the teeth which caressed her, but almost at the same time, Odette's tongue replaced the teeth and that clever tongue at once ascertained the accuracy of Florence's statement, and that if she was no longer a virgin, her maidenhead was still intact.

As for Florence she experienced all the pleasure which can be given by a skilful tongue, and it was so intense that she could hardly help uttering little shrieks as if in pain. She was almost in a swoon when the Countess began giving her on the mouth kisses which had been so profusely distributed elsewhere.

"Ah! it is my turn!" she said in a state of great excitement.

And she let herself glide from the bed in the posture of the wounded gladiator. The Countess took her place on the bed and drew her body close to Florence's inclined head.

"Ah!" she murmured: "If a man had seen and heard what you just heard and saw, I should never dare to lift up my head again."

At that very moment the Countess was so close to her that her hair brushed Florence's head.

The beautiful actress gave a start, her nostrils quivered; she raised her head, opened her eyes, and perceived that her mouth was close to that fiery bouquet which at first sight had so excited her.

But the ardour of her desires had abated, and Florence, slightly tired, but not satiated, had now more leisure to devote to pleasure. She fondly kissed the perfumed hair and began returning the caresses which the Countess had lavished upon her; but suddenly she seemed struck with a novel idea, and, laying the Countess at full length on the bed, she applied her mouth to the latter's parted thighs, whilst she placed herself in a similar but reversed position.

Then the two bodies became one-the breasts were pressed on the respective bellies. During some moments all conversation ceased, for the two eager mouths were at work; nothing could be heard but the panting respiration of the women and sighs of pleasure, and suddenly both became motionless, quite exhausted.

This time there was a protracted pause. Both seemed as if sleeping. At last both appeared to revive, and simultaneously exclaimed:

"Oh, what bliss!" then, quite panting, dishevelled, with languid eyes, weakened by their exertions, they slipped from the bed and lay down on a long and spacious couch.

"Ah! beautiful Florence! What pleasure you gave me!" said Odette.

"Well, I am so glad I found something new."

"Oh, darling! I thought I should die!"

"Then you had much pleasure?"

"Oh, yes; but I fancy that it cannot equal that which a man can give."

"Do you think, then that a man in that respect is our superior?"

"Indeed I do. We but light the fire. We do not put it out."

"Whereas man..."

"Ah! Man thoroughly stamps it out Luckily we have some inventions which supply the place of what nature refused us.

"Have you not heard of dildoes?"

"Is it a fact that such things really exist?"

"No doubt, have you never seen any?"

"Never!"

"Would you like to see one?"

"Indeed I should very much like to."

"Do you know the shape of a man's attributes?"

"As much as I could judge from statues."

"Not otherwise?"

"No."

"You have never seen a man?"

"Never!"

"Oh, then I shall be able in my turn to show you something new."

"Have you any?"

"Yes, of every description."

"Oh, let me see them."

"Wait a little then," said Odette, "I will fetch all my treasures."

"Can I go with you?"

"Come."

Odette took Florence to her dressing room and then, opening a secret drawer in her necessaries, she drew forth a casket and two cases like those used for pistols.

She brought forth the whole collection and laid it on the couch for inspection.

"First of all," said Odette, "I must show you the contents of the casket. The jewel which it encloses is not only a historical jewel, but also a work of art. It is said to be the production of the great Benvenuto Cellini."

Odette opened the casket of red velvet, and exhibited a true masterpiece of carved ivory.

This was an exact life-size reproduction of man's organs of

generation, and was altogether an admirable work of art. On one side of it were carved the lilies of France, and on the other side the three crescents of Diane de Poitiers.

No doubt this marvellous jewel had been the property of Monsieur de Saint Vallier's daughter, the widow of Monsieur de Breze and mistress of Francis I, and Henri II.

Florence examined it, with astonishment at first, then with curiosity, and finally with admiration. With astonishment, because it was the first time that she beheld and touched a. like object; with curiosity because she did not know how it worked; finally, with admiration, because Florence was a thorough artist, and it was a genuine work of art.

At the base of the instrument there was a cavity which came to view by unscrewing a portion of it, and that contained works almost as complicated as those of a clock, setting in motion a rod, which caused some liquid to spurt out in imitation of the natural process.

Florence was rather astonished, and wondered at the great size of the instrument, but the Countess, with a smile, replied by making some very elementary demonstrations and experiments. She applied the instrument to her own person, and so managed matters that in a short time it was altogether lost to view.

"You perceive how it works!" she said. "Yet you must confess that the receptacle is not apparently in proportion with its contents."

Florence leaned forward to make a closer inspection.

There was indeed no exaggeration. What the Countess stated was perfectly correct.

At first she put her hand to the appliance and moved it up and down.

"Not without milk!" said the Countess, staying her hand.

Having now sufficiently admired the historical jewel, they next inspected another, which was enclosed in one of the velvet cases. This was a common dildoe, of the same description as those manufactured in France or England, but more artistically made than those which were designed at the time for Italian and Spanish convents, where a couple of millions were sold every year.

This one was similar to that of Diane de Poitiers, of the ordinary size, about five or six inches in length and flesh-coloured, but the contrivance for the emission of the liquid was not so complicated; as this one was not so artistic as the first, the two women paid less attention to it than to the beautiful instrument which had had the honour of being used by Diane de Poitiers.

They now went on to the third. On beholding this Florence gave a shriek of surprise and terror. No wonder, for it measured from seven to eight inches in length and five or six in circumference.

"Oh!" said she. "That one is not of Diane's. It is rather of Pasiphae!"

The Countess laughed.

"Therefore do I call it 'The Giant'. It is a curiosity from South America and gives us an idea of what the requirements of the ladies of Rio de Janeiro, Caracas, Buenos Ayres and Lima may be."

"But see how marvellous are the works of this affair."

"Indeed it was a marvellous piece of workmanship, and was formed of some kind of gum highly-polished, each hair was set as if by one of the best hairdressers in Paris, and assuredly it had been cast, according to the practice of the sculptors, in a good mould from nature."

"Why," said Florence, who could not encompass it in her tiny hand. "This is a monster, and I do not believe there is a woman alive who could give a reception to such a huge thing."

Odette smiled, but said nothing.

"But do reply," said Florence, with impatience, "and do not laugh at me any more."

"I am not laughing at you, my little Florence," said Odette. "Now listen."

"I listen," said Florence.

"Should a woman wish to amuse herself with a jewel of that size, deliberately and without preliminary excitement, it could not be used without the greatest exertion, but supposing that two women mutually excite one another by all kinds of caresses, that the one who plays the lover, brings the other, the mistress to the highest pitch of salaciousness, she then applies the dildoe well coated with cold cream, and pushes it in gently, the thing will find an easy ingress and, once fairly home, will give the greatest possible pleasure."

"Impossible!"

"Will you make the experiment?"

"Who shall I try it on?"

"On myself."

"I shall split you open!"

"Am I split open?"

"Well; yes. Yes; I am willing," cried Florence.

"Wait a moment."

The Countess, who no doubt expected this event, had put some cream to warm in a small silver teapot on a spirit lamp.

She fetched the largest of the jewels, and drew from the same velvet bag an elastic belt.

"Come here," said she to Florence, with quivering nostrils that told their tale.

"Why?" inquired Florence, quite frightened.

"That I may make a man of you."

Florence drew near, the Countess encircled her waist with the belt, to which the dildoe was affixed in the proper position, and she placed in her hands the Renaissance jewel, prepared with lukewarm cream; then, kissing Florence, who trembled, and who now resembled a youth monstrously well treated by nature, she took off the counterpane and threw herself on the bed.

"Do what I tell you," said she, "and obey all my instructions."

"Have no fear," said Florence, as excited as the Countess. "If you told me to tear you open I would do it."

"Your mouth..."

Florence cast Diane's lover on the floor and began using her clever tongue to some purpose.

She felt this caress ought to vie with the rough caresses which were to ensue.

Odette replied with all the expressions of Lesbian tenderness. Florence was her friend, her angel, her heart, her life, her soul. The whole scale of sensual exclamations came one by one from her quivering lips, until, quite panting, she could only say: "Diane! Diane!"

Florence understood her, picked up the royal jewel, slipped it under her lips so there could be no interruption in the pleasure; and, in effect contrived in such a clever manner that the scale was unbroken, but went on with a new degree of intensity. Florence kept her eyes fixed on the jewel. She saw it enter; glide out. The Countess now did not speak, but only gave utterance to little shrieks. Suddenly she cried:

"The milk!...the milk!..."

Florence pressed the spring and a deep sigh showed that the Countess was experiencing the pleasure which is only given by coition, because that alone can satiate and calm. But the Countess knew that after this sensation another one was to come which only awaited the signal, and Florence in the midst of the plaintive ejaculations of her victim, made out the words: "The giant!... the giant!..."

Florence was expecting this request with impatience. The moment had come when she was to play her real part; she threw on the floor Diane's jewel, and began to play the part of a man with the greatest vigour. The Countess shrieked but strung herself up for the pain.

"Go-go on!... Oh! you are splitting me open! Go On! Ah! It is in!"

The Countess was not mistaken, it was indeed in, and the paroxysm of enjoyment was come. Then, quite maddened, she uttered cries of passion, shrieks of rage, among which might be heard almost inarticulate requests:

"Your mouth... your tongue... take my breasts; kiss the nipples. Oh gracious! how nice it is! Now the spring... Ah! my handsome giant!... Again! Again! Again!"

At last the Countess begged for mercy. Florence unclasped the belt and let it fall to the floor with its appendage.

The Countess lay stretched out full length and motionless on the bed.

Florence felt half mad with excitement. She filled again the ivory jewel with milk; leant back in the easy chair, and inserted the end of the dildoe until it touched her maidenhead. But soon she perceived that in this posture she lost part of her strength; so she sought another. She placed two pillows side by side on the easy chair, on which she rested her elbow, and she began to use the jewel in a manner which gave evidence of her skill and long habit; she harmonized the motion of her loins with the progress of pleasure; then, feeling it coming, she pushed the instrument home, gave a shriek of pain and of pleasure, and, imparting to the royal jewel the necessary movements, she fell back, almost fainting away with the exquisite sensation.

The beautiful Countess sat up on the bed and looked with astonishment. The proud young woman had kept her word. She had sacrificed her virginity to herself and herself alone.

We were three days and three nights without seeing the Countess, and on the fourth day she came to say that Violette might begin her lessons with Florence. After a scene of jealousy very well acted by the Countess, Florence gave her word that she would never interfere with Violette, limiting her attention to the development of her natural talent.

The union of the two disciples of Lesbos was consecrated, and the Countess acquired a marked liking for her new relations, without, however, in any way neglecting Violette, who for a long time continued in her studies with Florence and made a very successful debut.

Our delightful life of love thus went on for a few years; then, then... Ah! it is sad to say what happened. I wished to conclude here one of the most charming episodes of my existence. But since I have begun I must go to the end.

One evening, the Countess, who was always ready to take Violette away from me, found means to keep her in her box after a reception.

The child caught cold and began to cough. This was neglected. She became seriously ill, and as she seemed more excitable since her illness we loved one another too well, in spite of the remonstrance's of the doctor and with the natural consequences.

She was very ill during the winter, lingered on through the summer, and when the autumn leaves began to strew the ground, we accompanied poor little Violette to her last resting-place.

Before expiring she had taken me in her arms, saying: "My own Christian, I love you."

I had a large glass bell placed over her grave, and underneath the Countess and myself planted some of the flowers which had given her a name. For a long time we mourned her loss. Then Florence's love on the one side, and the incidents of everyday life on the other, effaced little by little the bitter recollection of the supreme parting.

I even forgot on the anniversary of her death to go and gather the tiny flowers, the roots of which fed on the substance of my beloved little mistress.

The Countess was more faithful to the memory of poor Violette, and sometimes sent me the flowers with but one word:

"Ungrateful man!"

And now that the story of our short-lived love has come to an end, I have nothing more to do than roll up my MS., tie it up, and, happen what may, I throw it at random on the desk of some intelligent publisher who may be clever enough to catch it up.

Sweet Seventeen

Sweet Seventeen: the True Story of a Daughter's Awful Whipping and its Delightful if Direful Consequence
Anonymous

What is there in the air of Paris which leads us all on to excesses of erotic appetite? Why is sensual gratification the be-all and end-all of the dwellers in the French capital, not dubbed the "Gay City" for nothing?

The atmosphere is transparently clear; the climate is relaxing. Most of the Parisian females are anaemic, and their nerves get the upper hand.

Is it the same with the males, perchance in a lesser degree, so that we may diffidently put forward the hypothesis that neuropaths predominate in the population of the pretty town?

There is not the slightest doubt, be the reasons what they may, that the craving for copulation takes hold of the most frigid individuals of both sexes when once they live within the Lutetian walls.

Oliver Sandcross, born and bred in London, was a splendid example of our bold sweeping theory. Here was an English gentleman, well brought up, and a noted engineer, rather pious too- that is the extraordinary part of it all-who developed the most satyr-like tastes when he settled down in Paris, with his wife and only child, a daughter. The capricious fairy, electricity, whose secrets have only been but slightly fathomed in the last few years, had tempted staid Oliver, and he became one of the most ardent seekers after the advantages to be gained in subjugating this new force. Brilliant offers, relating to lighting and tramways, had caused him to take up his residence in Paris, where, originally wealthy, he made more money than he knew what to do with.

Soon after his arrival, his religious habits dropped away from him, and after business hours he found the greatest pleasure and delight in hunting for feminine prey among venal beauties of all ranks. He admitted every specimen to the album of his fancy, from the married woman, met with at friends' houses and received in his own, to the short-skirted, twelve-year-old flower-girl of the Boulevards. Of the intermediate stages on the rungs of the ladder of lust, it would take us too long to talk, although a classification of Paris prostitution would be a tempting task for the student of psychopathy-if indeed it were possible to establish in schematic form the odds and ends of masculine and feminine humanity which go to make up the alluring and ever-changing kaleidoscope of Paris "on the loose".

Mr. Sandcross had tried everything in turns and nothing long, and his libidinous, almost insensate curiosity had led him to essay what new joys could be found in the depilated arms of effeminate, degenerate lads; some who had proposed themselves to the merry, rich Englishman in good society and others fresh from the workbench, selling their half-starved bodies for pocket-money. In justice to our sturdy Anglo-Saxon, we hasten to state that Socratic vice did not hold him long. His curiosity glutted, he returned to lavish his money on the petticoated little animals who are said to rule the world because their hands rock the cradle. But we think their domination arises from the fact of us men placing our sceptre in their adroit fingers.

Oliver Sandcross confessed to forty-seven years of age when he first came to live in France, a few years ago, and he was a fine specimen of a fifty-year-old rake. He was fair, bald, with a florid complexion and a brown beard rapidly getting white; not too tall; very stout; fine eyes, and a fleshy mouth moist with lechery and full of real sound teeth. In fact, the type of an arthritic, healthy, athletic voluptuary, full of energetic lewdness, with only room in his brain for two hobbies: electricity, with which he obtained gold, and voluptuousness which led him to scatter the yellow coins broadcast.

There was nothing to check him in his lustful career. Moral scruples he had none, remorse and repentance had been left on the threshold of the last church he had frequented, and his wife, luckily for him, never troubled him. She was a pure-minded English gentlewoman, very pretty, and full of love for her husband. She swore by him, adored him, tended him, and he comprised the whole world for her. There was plenty of jealousy in her composition, but it had never been aroused, because nothing could shake her faith in her Oliver. He was the soul of honour in her eyes, incapable of telling a lie or doing a mean action. Had Mrs. Sandcross found her lord in the arms of another woman, she would have turned away from the disgusting sight, merely marvelling at the wonderful resemblance to her husband of the man she had seen. Her good, kind female friends, following the promptings of Christian duty, had tried to perform the mischievous operation known "as opening her eyes". They had all signally failed, for the simple reason that this confiding helpmate did not really understand their perfidious innuendoes. One and all came to the ultimate conclusion that Mrs. Sandcross was either a born fool, or else she shut her eyes to her husband's "goings-on, and therefore they left her to enjoy a life of felicity in her fool's paradise. She was indeed a most happy woman, bathing in daily delight between the attentions of her kind husband, who was generous to a fault, careful, and thoughtful; grateful at not being troubled by the woman who bore his name and looked after his household, and the unceasing devotion of her handsome daughter.

No lovelier creature, no more perfect picture of a graceful English virgin could have been seen than Fanny Sandcross, the petted offspring of a lewd father and an indulgent mother. Miss Sandcross was tall-too tall, said hypercritical observers-overtopping her father by an inch or two. But what perfection of form; firm bust; tiny waist; swelling hips; massive spherical posteriors; wee feet and hands; satin, fair skin; masses of auburn hair; a tip-tilted, thoroughly Anglo-Saxon nose; with rose-leaf nostrils palpitating at the least emotion; a small mouth with pulpy red lips, and her father's perfect dentition. Her eyes would have been nearly sufficient to cause her to be adored even were her other charms less overpowering. They were blue, grey, or violet; according to the light, or the ideas of colour of the person who looked at her, but we should say they were of the last-named rare hue. Shaded with long lashes and surmounted by arched brows, they were full of ever-changing expression, but what dominated was a look of almost babyish curiosity. She seemed always as if just born to the world and its mysteries; as if interrogating her interlocutor and begging him to tell her something more; some fact that he might be hiding from her. Fanny gave the impression of perfect innocence and purity, and her portrait when she was eighteen would have formed a model embodiment of unspoiled girlhood.

It is far from wonderful for a maid to conduct herself with all the artlessness of a sweet angelic creature as yet unsullied by the least polluting contact; guarded by vigilant parents from surroundings calculated to tarnish the mirror of her virtue, but what was miraculous in the case of the beautiful Miss Sandcross was that she knew everything that a young girl of eighteen should not know. The more her terrible precocious insight into the secrets of sex increased, the more artless was her bearing. Some ancient Puritan strain must have caused her naturally to be able to touch pitch with an outward semblance of undefiled sinlessness which we may mention at once never left her all her life.

When we say her cognisance of forbidden subjects was peculiar and extensive, it must be understood that she was fully enlightened on all womanly mysteries, and there was no vice of venery which she could not catalogue, but her comprehension of the lascivious list of the hidden vices of humanity was far from being categorically formulated in her budding brain. What she knew, she had heard about and read about, but it had not yet taken a real shape in her mind. She was like a young lad revelling in the perusal of military history and bloody battles, but quite unable to realize the horrors of warfare and its saddening results.

This young damsel had been initiated in a very simple manner. When she came to Paris with her parents, she was eighteen and fresh from an English select academy for young ladies. Her mother, wrapped up in her husband and her own comforts, never troubled about her daughter's inner consciousness. It was true she would not allow her Fanny to be exposed to the contamination of a French school and took care to have her education terminated at home, by the aid of governesses. Miss Sand-cross was exceedingly quick and intelligent, and would soon have been able to teach her teachers. Her English and French were perfection; she had a smattering of German and Italian; and was a natural pianist and a fair singer. But the ladies who came to give her lessons were retained, more as companions for her, or chaperons, as it is an inflexible unwritten law that no single girl can be allowed to go about Paris alone.

The governesses were often changed. They underwent two distinct ordeals. First of all, their sweet young pupil pumped them as dry as she could, never ceasing to ply them with questions relating to tabooed topics: matrimony and kindred matters. Secondly, if they were at all well-favoured and desirous of keeping their situation, they had to submit to Mr. Sandcross's caresses. If they were virtuous they did not remain long in the rich electrician's flat; being unwilling to answer the daughter's queer queries, and revolting at the father's rudeness.

These intrigues were unknown to the mother, but Fanny, without having any idea that her dear father had really possessed most of her governesses entirely, perceived clearly that he liked to flirt with them. Sand-cross was really very excited over all the girls coming in contact with his daughter. It seemed to increase his enjoyment, when he thought that Fanny was constantly being attended by her father's mistresses. The knowledge that one of these lady companions went out to a matinee or concert with his daughter after a hasty upright encounter in his private den, without having had time to cleanse herself from the final spurt of his lubricity, lifted him far above the ordinary haven of debauchccs, and landed him into some celestial unknown space of aphrodisiacal ether.

From thence to falling madly in love with his own charming offspring was but a step, and he took it boldly, firmly, and resolutely. Fanny was eighteen when he woke up one fine morning and found out while having his bath that if he did not deflower his own flesh and blood, he would be most unhappy. He suddenly saw that he had been in love with her for a very long time, but did not realize his own passion. Now that he felt his bold longing tightly clutching his brain, it may be imagined that he tried in some way or another to try and overcome his unnatural desire, or fought against the criminal passion. Not at all. He never troubled so far, merely meaning to try and enjoy his own girl, if he could; and if he did not succeed-well, it would be time enough then to see what could be done. The fact is, so many women had dropped down before him, ready to place themselves in any posture that best pleased him, that he hardly fancied Fanny would resist him any more than the others. They were strangers. He had no influence over them, and yet their seduction was not difficult. How much more easy to allure and entice his own daughter, fond of pleasure-going, dress, and jewellery? Moreover, he felt sure she loved him, for he had been the best of fathers to her up to the present. At least, so he thought, according to his lights. He had made her his companion to a certain extent. His wife was lazy, fond of good cooking and novel-reading. She could manage a house very well, and keep servants in order, but when her daily task of organizing work and having meals properly cooked and punctually served was over, she was content to sink into an armchair and cry showers of tears over some silly tale of love. She was glad when her husband took Fanny out of an evening, and did not trouble about what time they came home or where they went. Thus it was that Miss Sandcross had gone with the author of her being to all the second-rate theatres where spicy comedies of adultery and salacious intrigue are played. The variety halls had no mysteries for her. She sat unconcerned in the private boxes of the Folies-Decolletees, and her pa told her the latest echoes of the wings, concerning the amours of Juanita la Torticula, the lovely Spanish dancer who had formed a Lesbian liaison with Phyllis de Honiton, a high-kicking goddess starring at the same establishment. Mr. Sandcross did not say so in as many words to his pretty daughter, but when she put up her fan, as if to hide a blush, and nodded as much to say, "Yes, pa, I know!" he felt that his dear little Fanny was au fait. It did not seem strange to him that she should know what a cocotte was, or that she should have heard who kept such and such a notorious prostitute of Paris. His daughter was eighteen, and most girls at that age learnt from their companions what was what, didn't they?

He was not alarmed to see her devour the raciest of modern French pornographical novels, and he himself purchased and took home to her every week the "bluest" and broadest comic papers, where naked bosoms above, and well-filled embroidered drawers below give purchasers of the suggestive pictures scarcely anything to guess at between the lines and legs. The mother's listless-ness allowed Fanny's thoughts to run in a very muddy channel. The young lady was not corrupted, because there was nothing to corrupt. Her perversity was natural, she was born that way, and her licentious predisposition was encouraged, instead of being toned down by proper home life and true womanly aspirations.

After the theatre, dressed in the height of fashion, wearing costly diamond rings and beautiful jewellery, all given to her by her doting father, Fanny, radiant in her tight-fitting frock and picture-hat, would sup tête-à-tête with her papa in the public room of some swell restaurant, where the tziganes played, and high-class painted beauties in society and of the half-world, assembled to carry on the business of selling their bodies to the highest bidder, strictly without reserve.

When next day, Sandcross was complimented by acquaintances on the comeliness of the lovely young girl supping with him the night before, he would, according to his humour, smile and change the subject, or maybe tell his friends it was his daughter. When they refused to believe him, perfectly certain that no self-respecting parent would take his daughter to places which after all were little better than common night houses, and chuckling, call him a sly dog, our prodigal father was delighted and would laugh at the joke with Fanny when he got home.

When his carnal craving suddenly arose in his being and he resolved to try and seduce his daughter, he turned the matter over in his mind and saw that he had very little more to do, having unconsciously prepared her for her fall ever since she had attained the age of puberty.

More books for her to read, perhaps a little stronger, if he could obtain anything more tropical without being downright bawdy; a few finer finger rings; a new dress or two; boxes for first nights and suppers at the most brilliant resorts. What more could he do? He would try kisses and sly touches to arouse her passion.

At this moment Fanny was eighteen and papa got his wife to imagine that it was she herself who had decided that their daughter needed no governess. She could go out with her music-mistress now and again; with lady friends or her mamma; by herself in the motor-car, or in a taxi, but never on foot-and after all was he not there to take her out with him, if she got dull, now and again? Mrs. Sandcross, as usual, was pleased to find her paragon of a husband good enough to trouble himself about his daughter, until she got married. Mr. Sandcross frowned as he heard the last word, curtly saying he would see all about that in good time, and leaving his better half, he took Fanny out to a music-hall where a very smutty revue was being played. The actresses wore no shoulder-straps to their low-necked costumes, and he liked to see his daughter blush, when the brazen hussies showed the slobbering stallites the black bouquets of their armpits.

It was not the first time by far that the father and daughter had gone to spend the evening at a place of entertainment, but Sandcross had never experienced the sharp pangs of lustful yearning that thrilled him on this occasion. He had indulged in extra wine at dinner at home, and towards the end of the repast had called for a bottle of champagne to be uncorked, of which Fanny had partaken.

In the carriage her sapphire orbs were sparkling with rays of light. She felt jolly and told her father so. He replied by placing his arm round her waist and kissing her cheek. She was not surprised; he often did so. But she did think he was really too affectionate that evening, for he kept his arm behind her all the way to the music-hall, and his face was near her shoulder. He eagerly inhaled the natural, sweet fragrance arising from her full frame, and regretted that the scent which she used so liberally half effaced the true perfume of womankind. Sandcross made remarks on his daughter's dress, criticising the fit of the corsage, enabling him to pass his feverish trembling ringers over her proudly swelling breasts, until she pushed his hand away with a laugh, telling her pa how ticklish she was. It must not be thought that she had the slightest lascivious feelings while her papa tried to tousle her as much as he dared, not wishing to disarrange her toilette in the cramped carriage, for despite all her enlightenment, or perhaps because of her comprehension of sensual secrets, she had as yet never experienced the slightest thrill of melting consciousness in the innermost recesses of her temple of love.

She only thought her father was quite too awfully tender-hearted when he had enjoyed a good dinner and an extra glass of wine.

All the evening, in the private box, papa sat close behind her. She felt his hot breath on her neck and ears; and his knees pressed into her hard buttocks as they fully covered the seat of her chair. At every obscene joke, his elbow nudged her, or he touched her arm. She smiled at him archly, but would quickly open her fan, or take up her glasses with a vacant air of infantile wonderment.

She was greatly admired, and Sandcross revelled in the

atmosphere of admiration environing his offspring. Between the acts, men in faultless evening dress came and stood in front of the box, twisting their moustaches, shooting out their cuffs, and trying to ogle her, some timidly, others with bold, offensive effrontery. Then she was full of joy, as she felt coming towards her the ardent desire of these libidinous men about town. They all wanted her; she knew it and felt it, her pretty little nostrils fluttering as she inhaled the invisible incense of their exasperated manhood. She knew too that they had no thought of pure affection, or devotion in the state of matrimony. Fanny was aware that their eyes were undressing her and the idea that they all longed to see her naked and wanted to get into bed with her to accomplish that mysterious penetration which it appeared was so delightful, made her heart beat with a sensation of great rapture, as she coolly noted the combined effects of her beauty, tasteful dress, and fine eyes. Other feelings, deeper and more intoxicating, would doubtless come soon, once Pygmalion should appear to animate the organs of her sex with the sacred spark of pleasure, but at present all was dormant in her grotto of Venus.

In the motor-car, papa was still more pressing. He talked of the actresses on the stage, of the be-jewelled harlots in the auditorium, and compared their charms with those of his daughter. The leading lady in the obscene play they had just witnessed was not so well made as my darling, Mr. Sandcross remarked. She was too fat here, and not well pulled in there; while as for her thighs, they were as thick almost at the knee as up here, and at every "here" and "there," his hands pinched, pressed and patted the corresponding parts of his own girl's body, but she only languidly pushed his encroaching fingers away with a gesture of impatience.

They had a supper at a restaurant which kept open all night, and where an orchestra started playing when the theatres closed. All the tables were engaged by noted whores, and catalogued and classified married women; leaders of feminine fashion, who were known for their long retinues of lovers, their openly avowed normal vices, and their scarcely hidden abnormal tastes.

A gorgeous female of about thirty-five years of age was supping at a table opposite them and she never took her eyes off lovely Fanny. Sandcross saw the languid imploring glances directed at his daughter and called her attention to the insistent leer of the painted lady. Miss Sandcross stared at her papa with widely opened eyes and coolly replied that she had seen and noted everything.

"She showed me the end of her tongue just now-the silly creature!" said Fanny. "Wouldn't you have liked to have seen her doing that?"

"Yes, indeed I would!" replied Sandcross, drinking a second petit verre. "Try and get her on again. Smile at her a little, Fan, and perhaps she'll do it once more. She's dying to kiss you, you know!"

"Don't be so stupid, pa!" replied Miss Sandcross, coldly and scornfully, but without a blush or a movement either of approval or disgust. "Wouldn't it be better to pay and go at once? It's awfully late and these people will be getting noisy soon and begin to throw things at each other as usual. And you'll be incapable of conducting me out of here, for if we don't hurry I shall have to carry you myself!"

Papa, always attentive to the smallest wish of his adored girl, soon led her to the car, and held her tight to him all the way home. He was dying to kiss her, but did not dare. Fanny merely said that he was a most horrible papa when he was tipsy, and sat quietly half asleep, yawning now and again, one hemisphere of her splendid backside resting on his knee, while his left arm encircled her waist, his hand clasped over her left breast, and his lips almost touching her right ear.

All was quiet when they reached the sumptuous flat of the Boulevard Haussmann where Mr. Sandcross lived. The servants were on the sixth floor according to the custom in Paris, and Mrs. Sandcross was fast asleep, having eaten too much-gormandising was her only vice- snoring heavily in her own room, for her husband had long since slept away from her for reasons that can be well understood.

Fanny was tired and dying to get to bed, although her father wished her to sit with him a little while in the dining-room, while he mixed himself a whisky and soda. She refused and left him. He wanted to kiss her as she said good-night, but she demurred with a laugh, saying that he had embraced her enough that evening, and pirouetting saucily, retired to her own chamber.

Sandcross stood erect in the middle of the room, staring after her. He trembled with lust and undefined desire; the blood rushing to his head and obscuring his vision. She must be his. None but he should possess her. But how and when? He knew from his experience of womankind that she had as yet no real feelings of sensual excitement, and there was little chance that he as her father would ever be able to arouse them. Yet he longed for her, and the thought of the crime he was meditating never once entered his mind. There was no thought of enjoyment increased by incest such as might have struck some worn-out debauchee. He loved Fanny with all the strength of his soul, and he had never felt like this with any other woman. It was his first love and his last.

"She must be mine, by God!" he exclaimed, half aloud, his heart beating, and a hundred hammers tapping inside his skull, as he cautiously crept towards Fanny's room and knocked lightly. In reply to her request to know who was there, her papa replied:

"It's all right! Let me in, I want to speak to you."

Recognizing her father's voice, she opened the door and he entered quickly.

Fanny had already begun to disrobe, having taken off her dress. She was in her stays of light blue satin. They were very short, forming almost only a girdle and her large breasts could nearly be viewed entirely, nestling in the lace insertions of her chemise, which was also ornamented with narrow turquoise ribbon tied under her round globes in front, in the style of the gowns of the First Empire. She wore a short petticoat of white chiffon, and mouse-coloured silk stockings to match her little high-heeled suede leather low shoes. Her magnificent hair was tumbling about her shoulders, and as she stood beneath the white glare of her electric lamps, facing her father, who trembled in front of her, his features crimson with excitement, she was indeed a marvellous type of youthful beauty and in a few years all men would be at her feet.

"I can't find the key of the Tantalus, my girl!" said her father, huskily.

"I'm sure I don't know what's become of it! I never have it, pa!"

Sandcross fidgeted a little and then turned as if to go.

"Well, I suppose I must do without my whisky tonight." He stopped short, looking about him. "This is a nice comfortable room, and you have arranged it with great taste. There are your books, and your drawings- and what a lot of knick-knacks and souvenirs! Aren't you afraid of breaking them?"

Fanny did not seem to trouble much about her pa's questions, thinking he was very tiresome that evening, and she sat down and began to pull off her shoes.

Sandcross came to her, and stroked her luxuriant tresses. "What lovely hair! How well it looks on your shoulders! How long it is!" He stroked her bare shoulder and patted her plump, naked arms.

"Aren't you going to bed tonight, pa?" rejoined Fanny, with a laugh which terminated in a yawn.

Sandcross, breathing heavily, bent his scarlet face near hers.

"Yes, Fan. Don't you bother. Give me a kiss!"

"You are a tease! Well, there! I'll kiss you goodnight and then you must go!"

She turned her face towards his, and he threw his arm round her neck, pressing his lips to hers in the most lewd manner. His fleshy mouth was half open and he thrust his tongue boldly in between her parted ripe lips, taking her quite by surprise.

She dragged herself away from him, with a movement of unutterable disgust thrilling through her entire body. Never had she been embraced in this vile way. Here was something she did not know after all. Kisses she had read about often, and knew that loving couples "glued" their lips together, but the insertion of a man's hot tongue in her cool mouth, choking her with wine and tobacco-flavoured, burning breath was too unutterably horrible. And then it was her father's mouth too! Was he mad or drunk? A sickening qualm caused the twin snowy mountains in her stays to rise and fall rapidly as she retreated to her bed, and placing her back to it, exclaimed, as she frantically wiped her lips with her hand:

"Oh papa! How dirty of you!"

But as she glanced at him, she noticed the horrible grimace of coming concupiscence that twisted his lineaments awry; his dilated revulsed eyes; a speck of white foam at the corner of his mouth-and a flood of light burst in upon her brain. She knew at last! He desired the enjoyment and possession of her body also-he, like the rest of the men, hungered for her-he, her father!

"You filthy beast!" she gasped, her eyes flashing disgust.

Deaf to everything save the promptings of unnatural carnality, he advanced towards Fanny, his arms outstretched, as if to seize her.

"I've longed for that kiss for years. I must have your lips again!"

95

Quick as lightning, she threw out her right arm and struck him full in the face, marking his cheek with the vermilion imprint of her lithe fingers.

Mad with rage and disappointment; furious to have to see the loathing scorn on the face of the beautiful daughter he adored, he rushed towards her with a guttural cry of mingled vexation and pain at the smart of the stinging slap. Throwing her on the bed face downwards, he held her firmly there, despite her struggles, pulling up her petticoat and casting it over her loins.

"Let me alone!" she murmured, struggling violently. "I'll rouse the house and call for ma!"

"I defy you to, hussy! You know how your mother believes in me! I'll lie to her and say you called me to your bed. You dare not do what you say-you would kill her! I'm going to punish you for your assault on me!"

He exposed the swelling expanse of her rotund posteriors, pulling at the cambric drawers which matched her chemise, and dragging them down to her heels.

She was too amazed and frightened to cry out, and indeed she feared the terrible scandal that would arise if she woke her mother. Before she had time to come to a resolution, or put her wildly scattered thoughts in order, a resounding slap from her enraged papa's open hand fell on the right cheek of her majestic bottom.

"Enough, father! Don't disgrace me! How dare you strip me like this?"

"Hold your tongue, hussy!" he replied, in a thick whisper, as he spanked the whole surface of her posteriors as hard as he could, reddening them all over. "You're my child, and you must obey me! I'll crush your pride!"

Delirious with lust and erotic rage; gloating over the sight of his desired daughter's naked flesh; revelling in the touch of his feverish palm on her smooth skin, he beat her with his hand until her backside was swollen and of a dark-brown hue. She writhed and moaned, sobbing hysterically, but biting the blanket so as to stifle her cries.

His right hand ached, and having regained his self-possession in some slight degree, he crossed over and struck at her tortured bum with his left.

"Oh! papa, do let me go! It burns! You do hurt me so dreadfully!

Oh! Oh! Ah!"

"This is nothing, my beauty!" said Sandcross, with a laugh. "Tomorrow I'll get a rod, and a whip, and flog you within an inch of your life! I'll teach you to disobey your poor old father! Take that, miss; and that; and that!"

Again the remorseless hands fell with greater force than ever, raising little blue bumps here and there in the brown shading that obscured her queenly hinder beauties.

"Oh! Oh, papa! What humiliation! Do please leave off! Turn out the light! Don't look at me all bare-oh! ah! Don't-don't hit me any more!"

"Will-you-be-quiet?" retorted her father, striking fiercely and slowly at each word. "Missy don't like the humiliation, don't she? Ha! ha! I can see your bottom and your thighs-yes, your naked thighs, dear, and your pretty calves and feet!"

Despite his coarse utterances, he did not forget to still batter her martyred bottom with all his might, and the skin being of the finest texture now began to break. Little streaks of blood appeared, oozing out in different directions from the raised bruises which turned black.

Low moans issued from her throat. She writhed and twisted in all directions, once placing her hands behind her in a futile attempt to protect her buttocks. Sand-cross struck at her wrists and she hurriedly drew her arms away.

"Enough, papa! Enough!"

"Beg my pardon!" said Sandcross, as he now inflicted swinging blows at her hitherto untouched thighs.

"Not there! Not there, papa!"

"Will-you-beg-my-pardon? I'll hit you where I like! I'll strip you naked and flay you alive, if I choose! Am I not your father?"

"Yes! Y-e-e-s-pa! I beg your pardon-I do indeed!"

She was now quite subdued and conquered, reclining quietly on her stomach, her body wriggling from side to side, and heaving her buttocks up and down. She sighed heavily, and muffled sobs came from between her ringers, as she now clasped her hands before her face.

"Promise to kiss me of your own free will and I'll let you off!" said the cruel father, as he contemplated with lewd joy Fanny's reddened, fat thighs.

From her loins to the tops of her stockings, not an inch of skin had escaped the effects of Sandcross's awful punishment. All was red, contused, of a reddish-brown tint, and on the buttocks the skin was broken; bleeding in many places.

Fanny's father waited for an answer, as he finally desisted. He was fatigued, both his hands were benumbed, and he felt quite exhausted, but happy, with a glorious exciting inward upheaval of satisfaction. The pleasure of cruel conquest; the delight at having crushed the rebellious spirit of the daughter he coveted was something too great for words to qualify.

His girl's reply came at last, and in such a fashion as to thoroughly surprise him.

She slowly turned round, unable to rise entirely from the bed, and utterly regardless of the indecency of her posture, as she showed fully three-quarters of the front part of her body; her breasts escaping from her twisted stays, the nipple-buds showing above the lace-trimmed edge; her drawers disarranged in front, exposing part of her virgin soft fleece, she held out her arms to her father, and through the tears that veiled the lustre of her eyes, a glorious smile lit up her tearful face. She murmured in French, couched in a low, loving whisper:

"Viens! Prends-moi! Prends-moi! Je t'aimc!"

His brain reeling, every nerve thrilling, and a prey to rampant, ungovernable lust, Sandcross threw himself on his daughter. His mouth sought hers, and their tongues met in a libidinous, long, luscious caress. He rolled upon the bed grasping her willing body, and pressing her close to him. They neither spoke, but the father groaned with exacerbated longing, and his daughter gave forth deep sighs of satisfaction. While their mouths were joined, the profligate parent's hands eagerly pressed every bit of naked flesh he could find: the neck, chest, and the upper halves of the beautiful hard breasts heaving by reason of the tempest within; the burning backside and thighs; arms, hands, and hair. He plunged his fingers into the waves of her tresses, and even passed their tips over her face. Would their mouths never separate? They bit and sucked each other's lips, and Sandcross was intoxicated with her velvet saliva, fragrant and fresh.

"Love me, Fan! Love me and let me love you!" he whispered at length, as he sucked and bit at her well-formed, tiny ears, brilliant as pink pearls.

"I love you, pa! You know I do!"

Sandcross fingered at her stays. She disengaged herself from his arms for a second, and unclasping the busk, threw the corset behind her. With insane delight, her father pressed the hard globes, and found both nipples erect. He pulled down the chemise to kiss and lick the twin strawberries, one by one. While he did so, she dragged her arms out of the straps of her filmy garment, and was about to unfasten her petticoat and drawers, when the sucking caress of Sandcross produced the effect he wished, and with a lowing, loving, cooing sound, she fell on his lips again. He tugged at her petticoat. She understood, drawing it off and her drawers too. She was naked with the exception of stockings and shoes. He stood her up erect, admiring her unveiled frame, worthy of being copied in marble, and falling on his knees before her, kissed her thighs, and passed the end of his tongue through the mossy bush that concealed the sign of her sex. She clipped her legs fast together at this soft embrace, and placing her hand on his face, tried to close his eyes with her soft palm. Weak with the awaken-encroaching feelings of lust that racked her virginal body, she fell over him, about to faint with rapture, from the effects of the wave of unknown voluptuous sensations submerging her being. He lifted her up and threw her gently on her back on the bed, her legs dangling over the edge. Standing between her unresisting thighs, he parted them widely. His trembling digits tore at his trousers and braces. He felt that if he tarried but another second or two, nature would betray him. Hastily clutching a towel from the horse on his left, he lifted up his girl, and slipped it under her. She reclined with closed lids, one arm flung over her face, to hide it, and protect her eyes from the strong, searching electric light which made her white body look whiter still. He threw himself upon her. This contact caused her to shudder with delight, and fresh elixir sprung from her hidden source of future motherhood. She pushed up to meet the coming onslaught. Her sex prompted her, but she did not know what was in store for her, as she held out her arms to her father. He bent down and she clasped him to her breast, seeking always for his mouth. His tongue gambolled with hers. Now she shrank from him, and bit her left wrist to stifle her groan of pain. He held her fast now and gained at each powerful thrust. She writhed in agony, and was no longer moist. He panted with delight, feeling the commencement of his climax.

He fell on her breast, exhausted, half unconscious swimming in a sea of satisfied lewd joy, while Fanny sobbed partly in exquisite agony, and feeling a rending pain in each groin.

Sandcross rose at last, and drew the towel, now stained with blood, between her legs, trying to wipe the ensanguined secret recess. This caused her to sit up, and she hid her tearful face on her father's breast.

Now only did he feel a little uneasy. The door was actually ajar. They might have been heard? No, all was quiet. He whispered to Fanny to move gently from the bed, and placed her on the bidet. He kissed the toilet napkin with its scarlet spots, and she smiled through her tears while he did so, and as she saw him fold it up and place it in his pocket. She was not surprised, nor disgusted at seeing her father thus standing before her, his gradually shrinking instrument shamelessly dangling before her eyes.

"Do you forgive me?" he said, one tiny ray of remorse -the first and last-illumining the depths of his soul, obscured by the black clouds of incestuous lust.

"Yes, father. I love you! I regret nothing. I only want you to love me always!"

"Hush, Fan!" he rejoined, fearful as she raised her voice in her excitement. "I swear never to fail you. You're mine, doubly so, by mutual love and right of relationship. Trust in me and your life shall be one dream of happiness."

And so they kissed again. He put her in bed and tucked her up comfortably, whispering how he had done that when she was a tiny little baby girlie. She smiled at him, gratefully and happy as an angel, as he enquired if she was in pain.

"Down there-you know, pa-between my thighs- legs, I mean. And behind too! Oh! how you hurt me! I never knew your hands were so hard!"

"Poor girl! I'll never slap you again!"

"Oh yes, you may!"

In most childish confusion she threw her white tired arms around his neck, her lips skimming over his moustache, as she murmured: "I like it! It was that spanking which made me feel I loved you, darling pa!"

As her nervous system gradually reverted to its normal state of quietude, so the babyish look returned to her violet eyes, and her face was as full of innocence as heretofore.

"Good night, my own papa! Good night, dear love - my father-and my love!"

With a last kiss - a pure, chaste touch of her closed lips this time - she turned and slept like a child, sinking at once into hearty slumber.

Sandcross looked enraptured at her for a second, and switching off the light retired on tiptoe to his own room. Two or three times did he return in the night to kiss his loving girl, who still slept on, until he dared no longer show himself as the servants arrived through the kitchen at six o'clock.

Next day, Fanny stayed in bed, scolded tenderly for her love of theatres and suppers by her affectionate mother, although she could well understand the allurement of a coup of iced consommé and a truffle or two after the enjoyment of a new play.

The guilty couple now sailed on a calm and laughing lake of unmitigated wanton voluptuousness. Sandcross and his daughter lived through a perpetual honeymoon, and the electrician's wife was charmed to see such a perfect union, suspecting of course nothing whatever. A mother is always the last to grasp the guilt of her children. Sandcross's wife compared the life of their daughter with that of other girls in Paris; fretful, bickering, coquettish maidens, suffering from green sickness, and perpetually worrying their poor parents to get them a husband so that the wayward up-to-date damsels shall be at liberty to love - other men of their own choice.

Fanny grew exceptionally obedient and meek. Her chorus of "Yes, ma!" and "Yes, pa!" would have made the recording angel retire from business, had not the devil been there to whisper in his ear the secret of incestuous lechery that kept Fanny so outwardly calm. Indeed, when matrimony was mentioned it was she who consoled her mamma, impatient to see her daughter smothered in orange-blossoms and white faille.

"What are the men about?" she would sigh, and worry her husband to leave France, and settle in England, Saxon suitors not being so mercenary as the sons of Gaul.

In the meanwhile, Fanny and her father slipped into each other's rooms at night whenever it suited them, and that was very often.

From the point of view of simple salacity, it is perfectly certain that nothing can equal the enjoyment to be found with a young girl, really loving the man who has deflowered her. Her sensual being gradually develops in the arms of a male who is, for the time being, all in all to her-the one man in whom every thought and desire is centred. The surprises of slowly approaching womanhood, and the first thrills of ravishing, immodest pleasure and prurience have all arisen in her under his influence. She becomes his devoted slave, thankful for a kiss, and brimming over with gratitude for the deeper insidious final caress when he chooses to bestow it upon her.

There was another and more cynical standpoint which we must not forget, which will rejoice the heart of all those who find the power of their passions weirdly increased by inflicting punishment upon the object of their affections. To be able to hurt the loved one, mingling pleasure and pain at one's sweet will, certain that the dolent martyr will eagerly kiss the hand that brandishes the birch, is not that a most enchanting dream of overpowering delight?

Fanny's first sensual spasm was due to spanking, and the desire to be flogged would thus last all her life, inseparable from other yearnings. A young woman, whipped by her first lover, nearly always falls under the spell of the enchanted twigs. It seems as if the rod, red-hot, burnt into the brain, indelibly searing the imagination of the so-called victim. Such is the invisible brand of the birch.

Papa taught her everything that a woman could possibly require to know, especially those tit-bits of refined scientific stupration which females are generally better without. What a difference to the half-veiled semi-falsehoods of her silly governesses! Here was practice and theory.

What delighted Fanny most was Sandcross's staff of life itself; the tremendous instrument from which had sprung the mysterious germ of her existence. Alone with her father, she must need free the blind bird from its cage, and at rest, or proudly standing, it was unceasingly the object of her wondering admiration. She would play with it for hours, kissing it, talking to it, purring over it, examining it as if she saw it for the first time whenever her invidious hand dived deeply down in the folds of her father's underwear. When her eager, tickling touches caused her pa's excitement to bring him close to the goal of the orgasm, she fell back on his big hairy purse, playfully handling and dandling the slumbering olives which she deliriously exclaimed were her twin idols. She had sprung from their white foam like another Venus rising from a sea of sperm, and now they gave her the sole pleasure she hungered for in this world. How could she help worshipping them?

There was not the slightest shadow of repentance or remorse to darken the dazzling path leading through their waking dream of highly refined voluptuousness, and if it were possible for either of them to have given utterance to any inward prayer whatsoever, they would have lifted up their hearts in some song of touching, joyful thanksgiving to the unknown power that had created the daughter for the father, and the father for the daughter.

Fanny, by dint of perpetually playing a part, grew in time to be a most perfect actress and a ready, able, tricky liar. She gloried in her hypocrisy, and now and then amused herself by skating on the thinnest of ice, tempting Providence, and abandoning her mouth and body to the most shameless caresses, before her mother's back was scarcely turned.

Sandcross developed a new malady which he had invented himself-a kind of intermittent insomnia. He had irregular attacks of sleeplessness, enabling him to wander about the house at nights, and thus furnishing excuses for all noises and sounds of footsteps which might be heard in the small hours. His only cure was a glass of soda-water liberally dashed with spirits about two in the morning, with a cigar-and his wily, lustful daughter of the innocent violet eyes, to keep him company. She would then read to him chapters from ultra-naughty novels in French, English, and German, printed on the sly, and soon was a walking encyclopaedia of love, passion, and bawdiness. She rolled with radiant ecstasy in the slough of her shame, proud of being her own father's mistress, and always eager to learn fresh secrets of licentiousness.

In spite of all his scolding and alarms she would never permit him those exercises known to Malthusian couples as "withdrawing, nor practise any fraudulent tricks to hinder conception. Copulation, without the final shower of soft seed, she opined was like kissing a woman or a priest, something very nice, but detestably incomplete. If she fell in the family way, she declared she would retire to

Switzerland, or Belgium, and under a false name bring her dear baby into the world. She unblushingly declared to her father that she secretly longed to find herself enceinte, and would be pleased beyond measure to bear a boy, for preference, the picture she hoped of the dual father and grandfather.

Luckily her womb remained refractory, although she did all she could to bring about this consummation which her father devoutly wished would never take place.

Another of this extraordinary couple's delights was to take little trips alone together to most of the European capitals. Sandcross's business allowed him to travel as much as he liked; he had but to take the place of his representatives. By this means, he increased his gains and enjoyed his daughter more freely.

The rich Englishman and the young and lovely woman who was generally taken for his wife or mistress, had many strange little adventures together, seeing peculiar sights, as they always sought for some glorious indecency in all the capitals they visited. In Sweden and Norway, they had women to attend to them in their bath; in Russia, men assisted during their ablutions; and at Ostend, one day, on repairing to a bath-house, they were shown by the sedate proprietor into a double bathroom.

It must not be thought that Sandcross ever allowed any stranger to touch his daughter. He did not debauch her to that extent, nor did her insatiable curiosity for all the sights in the peep-show of sexual horrors induce her to forget her allegiance to her papa. She was an onlooker. She liked to see, but not to touch or be touched. We need not say more. The following instances will suffice to show our meaning.

Her father had been told that in Paris were miserable prostitutes of the lowest class, too old and ugly, or if young, too shabby, to show themselves in the light of day, and who eked out a precarious living by masturbating passers-by in the darkest recesses of the public parks and gardens. Fanny wanted to see these off-scourings of femininity, and her papa allowed her to view most smutty scenes.

There was a young creature dressed in bicycle costume, who with an old rusty machine, used to haunt the benches of the Bois de Boulogne. When in a lonely bypath, she espied a man on foot or on horseback, she would rise from her seat and open her bloomers in front showing the gaping, worn mystery of her shop-soiled sex. If this simple enticement succeeded, the sylvan siren drew her prey into the bushes and there offered him the contents of her breeches or the succour of her hands and mouth for a franc or two. She satisfied horsemen by standing on a bench or broad post, using her lips and mouth to sate their spending appetite, without it being necessary for them to dismount. Fanny saw her at work, and opened her baby eyes with her look of simplicity and candour, while the slow moisture of lickerish lewd desire on her glorious lips betrayed the secret concealed by her skirts, as she glanced at her father.

Their blood heated to boiling point, they would return to their taxi, stationed some little distance off, and Fanny would study the old legend of Saint George and the dragon, on pa's lap, greedily engulfing to the pommel the beloved sword that taught her mother the science of cut and thrust years ago, and which now urged on the daughter to her molten crisis of incest, assisted by the shaking of the hired vehicle.

Fanny would then sink down by Sandcross's side, happy and glutted, with her hand on the sign of virility. A black silk handkerchief was spread like an apron over the knees of the author of her being, and his private parts fully at liberty, his daughter could slip her hand underneath the dark foulard, and caress them as she chose while the wheels of their car rolled round. This was especially useful when going to the theatre or returning. Before reaching home, after the play they frequently indulged in complete connection in their roomy auto.

One cold November evening, at dusk, they strolled together through the Champs Elysees gardens, and Fanny dropping a thick, double veil, of the kind known in the trade astulle adultere, Sandcross interviewed a ragged young girl who was anxiously awaiting customers under the greenwood trees. A thick, rimy mist was falling, but the enterprising strumpet, in return for a trifle of silver, declared that she did not despair of getting enough to pay for her dinner and the morrow's keep in the course of an hour or so.

There are, it appears, a number of men who enjoy naught but the manipulation of female fingers in the open air. They stand up, and the woman plunges her hand into their trousers in front, or through an unstitched or cut pocket, according as these misguided voluptuaries of the highways have arranged. Some cast their seed upon the ground, like Onan of old, others preferring to ejaculate inside their garments. They like to walk away, feeling themselves bedewed with their own semen. Others only look at these girls busy in the dark. The wretched females know this well, and are not surprised when masturbating a client to see another ghostly masculine form looming up in the gloaming The male who is being operated may start, dismayed, and lose all the benefits of cheap al fresco massage, but the nymph of the Paphian groves of Paris, with her horny, but willing palm, reassures her idiot, telling him not to be alarmed but to hurry up and discharge, as the new arrival has only come to look on.

Sandcross and Fanny became lookers-on for once, and the father, always eager to please his daughter in her voyage round the world of venedy, told one of the open air, fingering females to accost the first passer-by and offer to masturbate him for nothing. Sandcross would treat the wayfarer to pastoral pleasure if allowed to look on with "his wife". Two or three men were induced to expose their persons, and the peripatetic harlot, delighted at the windfall, proved that she could play upon this pipe, it being as easy as lying down. While the men were being shaken and rubbed past the gates of paradise, Sandcross and Fanny stood by and compared proportions and form. Next, sodomitical storics sct the blood of Miss Sandcross on fire, and father and daughter watched the beardless boys of the unemployed stamp hanging about urinals offering their services to elderly, well-dressed men. Sandcross found out a furnished hotel, kept by a retired catamite, now too old to serve the inverted tastes of his patrons. He had invested his savings earned by the sweat of his brows in a comfortable little lodging-house, frequented by old friends and new acquaintances. Fanny and her father paid a visit there, and the jovial landlord at their request sent round the corner for a young passive pederast, who was celebrated for his abnormal proportions in one direction, and the narrowness of his... ideas, in another. The young knight of the powder puff appeared rouged, with hair dyed like that of a woman, wearing a loose, lay-down collar with a crushed strawberry cravat, and a short, tight-fitting, single-breasted jacket that enhanced the shape of his undulating crupper. Fanny thought she would have died of suppressed laughter when the grotesque hermaphrodite of the Boulevards walked with a wriggle of his breadwinner into the room and going straight up to Mr. Sandcross thrust his tongue into her father's mouth by way of polite salutation. The incestuous pair amused themselves by stripping and spanking him, and another boy being procured, they looked on while a pederastic duo was played from end to end for their benefit, not a note or variation being slurred over. When the lads were dismissed, Sandcross threw himself on willing Fanny and they fully satisfied themselves.

Such scenes were repeated for their benefit in many parts of France and other countries, Fanny never tiring. The nervis of Marseilles, the boatmen on the lakes of Northern- Italy, the gondoliers of Venice, the ragazzi of Rome, arid naked Neapolitans, all served to interest fantastic Fanny, the buxom queen of incest.

She increased in stature, and filled out, thriving on the rich libations of in-breeding, until she attained the massive, though proportionate curves of the Grecian Venus. Her existence was an ideal one. She loved but one man on earth. He returned her affection and was entirely faithful to her, thinking no more of any other female, and showering gifts on his daughter-concubine.

A cloud now passed over the happy home of Sandcross. His wife fell ill. Continuous gastronomical excesses, and a growing disinclination to put her foot to the ground or even go outside the house, had reduced Fanny's mother to the rank of an obese invalid. She developed rheumatic gout, and after several long illnesses and relapses, devotedly attended and nursed by her husband and daughter, it was discovered that her heart was touched and great care was therefore necessary.

Fanny was getting near the age of twenty, when the doctors gave their verdict, Mrs. Sandcross being convalescent after a more than usually painful crisis of her malady. She was ordered change of air; a season in her native country was the thing for her. So she went by easy stages to Buxton to spend the month of August and part of September in a hydropathic establishment. Fanny and her father accompanied her. All three were greatly fatigued; the sick woman and her two faithful nurses. Miss Sandcross was invited to stop with some friends at Pulborough in Sussex; and papa was forced to return to business in Paris. At that moment, he could not leave the capital for more than forty-eight hours at a time.

Papa and his Fan were greatly grieved at this their first separation, but they both needed rest and a change after the sleepless nights of anxious watching passed in turns by the bedside of the suffering mother.

About the middle of September, mamma was much better in health, though still rather weak, and she was allowed to depart from the sanatorium. Fanny's visit had come to an end and she was dying to be clasped to her father's arms once more. The Arcadian pleasures of honest English homes soon palled upon her, and she found the nights ridiculously long, as she tossed on her solitary spring mattress in the best guest room. She was courted and adulated by the finest young men one could wish to set eyes upon, gentlemen athletes, skilled in all sports and gentle as sucking-doves with the fair sex, but none of those who worshipped at the shrine of her beauty or fell stricken to the heart by the magic of her violet, marvelling orbs, made the slightest impression. She would have given all the picked lives at Pulborough and its vicinity for one, soft, lingering kiss from the parental lips. She loved her father deeply, truly, loyally.

Sandcross had arranged to go to England to fetch his wife and daughter, returning to France by way of Dieppe, meeting Fanny at Lewes as she left the Pulborough people, and proceeding to Newhaven with her, where father and daughter would meet Mrs. Sandcross returning from Buxton, and thus all three could embark and cross the Channel together.

All the dates were carefully arranged by Mr. Sandcross, and he had a motive in being so punctilious. He had not seen Fanny for nearly two months, and as he was getting on in years, full of business cares, and wary now of the wiles of professional prostituted beauties, we may surmise that he had been faithful to his own girl as he called her. He was burning for a quiet night with her, and had arranged things splendidly as he thought.

Mamma, of course, knew the day on which her husband would meet their daughter at Lewes, lunch with her there, and bring her on to Newhaven, but what she could not divine was that Fanny had arranged to leave Pulborough on the eve of the day notified to her mother, so as to get a night with her papa in the same bed, and then go on to Newhaven next morning. Sandcross was also to leave Paris twelve hours before the time stated to his wife. His good lady, rather feeble after her severe bout of illness, obliged to take minute doses of digitalis, thought it would be better to start from Buxton a day before the time fixed by her husband and sleep at Lewes. She really did not feel equal to going right through to Paris. It would be a nice little surprise, too, for Sandcross and Fanny when they met to have lunch, to find mama at Lewes having preceded them, instead of waiting their arrival at Newhaven.

The fun of her pleasant little trick sustained the poor lady on her journey, albeit she was but the shadow of her former self, walking and breathing with difficulty. She reached Lewes safely shortly after sunset and arrived at the specified hotel.

She asked for a room, and telling her name, explained how being unaccompanied, she wished to dine and sleep and meet her husband and daughter the next day. The reply came readily that Mr. Sandcross had just been in, had engaged the big room on the first floor for himself and lady, and had stepped out again.

Mrs. Sandcross, still really very ill, could not worry her enfeebled brain about this strange coincidence, and jumped at the muddled conclusion that somehow or the other she had misunderstood her husband's letter, which was in her reticule, and he was no doubt expecting her.

She replied with gasping utterances-it was strange now how the least excitement made her pant and tremble-that she was the lady in question, and would go up to her husband's room.

Once in the comfortable single-bedded, clean, old-fashioned chamber, she was glad to get off her hat and jacket and sit down to rest. There was a nice, antique, padded chair with big arms behind a light screen near the fireplace. She would recline there and have a nap until her good hubby returned. How she longed to see him and her handsome, devoted daughter! They were so good to her, so kind; such splendid nurses. The poor lady dropped a tear or two, partly out of pity for her own weakened, suffering self, and also for joy at being once more with the only two persons she loved. Really, she was very low and nervous. Doctors nowadays were great faddists. Fancy!-nothing but milk to live on for two months! No wonder she was all to pieces and starting at every sound. Wait until she got back to Paris. She would soon get her strength up with Normandy beef, grand fat fowls and fine old Bordeaux, not forgetting aged vintage

Champagne. It was time for another little sip of that nasty digitalis stuff, and she must read- hubby's letter-dear Oliver!-silly mistake-Sandcross always so particular too-doctors softening her brain- no more milk-so tired-my reticule. And Mrs. Sand-cross dozed peacefully in her comfortable armchair.

It was now dusk and the low-ceilinged room was full of deep shadow when Mr. Sandcross, escorting Fanny whom he had fetched at the railway station, came gently into the bedchamber.

The door was no sooner closed and locked than by a mutual impulse, they fell into each other's arms, upstanding, and their mouths met in a kiss of long pent-up desire, tongues intertwining, lips clipping lips, and hands clasped, until Sandcross threw his arms round her, moulding her buttocks with one hand while he pressed her close to him with the other so as to feel her perfect bust crushed and throbbing against his breast. They ceased for want of breath and lost no words in idle talk. Fanny left his clasp, took off her hat, and throwing her slight bolero behind her, began feverishly unhooking her bodice. Sandcross, congested, his outstretched hands trembling, stepped towards her. Fanny waved him off.

"Undress, pa darling! We shall just have time before dinner. Make haste, I'm longing for you much more than you are for me!"

With a merry smile of denial, Sandcross tore off all the armour of civilisation, but despite his celerity, Fanny was naked, save natty nut brown shoes and stockings, long before he had struggled out of laced boots and spun silk drawers.

He caught her again in his arms, drunk with delight as he once more felt her naked, tightly stretched, smooth skin against his sturdy, hairy body. The enamoured father would have dragged her to the bed, but she resisted.

"It will look so funny in this quaint hostelry if we go to bed before dinner. The sofa will suit, daddy love. I want to see you all over, and then you'll have to slap my bottom for being such a naughty little devil of a daughter as to play with the big thing I see sticking out from between my father's thighs. Oh! if it hadn't been for that great truncheon, I should never have seen the light of day, and also should never have had its whole length inside my body; in my hands; in my mouth- everywhere!-all over me!"

He was seated on the sofa, stark naked, and she, entirely nude too, was squatting between his open thighs admiring the gigantic, erect priapus she was so fond of. She caressed it with her fingers.

"Isn't it big? And impatient too? I can feel it throbbing in my hand. It feels for all the world like some huge, soft, warm dormouse that I might have made a prisoner. How nice you smell! What a time it is since I've enjoyed your own special perfume." She ceased stroking his standard in order to inhale the odour of her own fingers which she pressed rapturously to her nose.

"Come now, papa," said Fanny, excitedly, jumping up, "I've been a bad girl and have got so wicked." She took his hand and placed it on her. "You must punish me for that and drive all these naughty thoughts out of my head!"

She pulled him gaily off the sofa and threw herself upon it on her ivory belly.

Papa stood up over her, entranced with the sight of her sloping shoulders, arched loins and the immense expanse of her rotund buttocks, as white as driven snow and as elastic as a freshly-inflated balloon. He slapped quickly and smartly with deft, stinging, spanking blows due to long practice.

"Oh, it's beautiful! You make me feel so exquisitely naughty! Harder, pa, dear! Quicker, kill me! Strike more with the tip of your fingers! Oh! oh! No-no more! It's awful now! Not so fast! Am I red? Ah! That was too bad! I'm sure the skin is broken! Don't! Oh, don't, I tell you!"

She writhed and twisted, pressing one arm to her face, and the other was bent behind her, palm upwards, in the small of her back. Papa had never ceased cruelly beating her with his hands, first one, then the other, and finally both posteriors at once, until they were black and blue, irregularly studded with small speckled wounds, whence issued tiny drops of blood as big as pin-heads.

This was quite enough for brazen Fanny, who sprang up and threw herself on her back, placing her clasped hands about her papa's neck, and pulling him down to her. He fell heavily upon her. She opened her legs.

"Make haste, my own papa! Your daughter is dying for her father's hard cruel thing that tore her to pieces when she was eighteen! Oh, put it in! Quick! Give me all of it! Don't keep me waiting! Don't tease me so, pups!"

He was so excited and trembled so much with lust and long abstention from the pleasures of the flesh that he bungled.

"There-silly pa! You've forgotten how to do it! Was that how you managed with mamma? It's a wonder you ever got her in the family way at all then? Isn't it- oh!-how beautiful! Push! Now! There! Oh, don't come yet! Let me-spend-first! I'm spe-e-ending! Oh! oh! Stop, pa!"

He remained still, admiring her form, lifting himself up a little way, pressing her large breasts.

"Now, go on again Gently at first! So! Oh, papa! I'm your wife! Enjoy your wife, Oliver darling, and make her see the angels!"

"You're not my wife, Fanny child; you're my daughter, my own offspring, sprung from your old daddy's loins nearly nineteen years ago! Oh! oh! I can't help it! I must spend now!"

"I'm spending! Oh, papa-husband! Spend with me -now! Father, make me a baby! Not so hard, you'll spoil your little wifie!"

"Oh, Fanny! I'm spending! Oh, darling It's-too- much. Ugh There There! It burns me!"

He dropped flat on her body, stifling her cries with the pressure of his hot mouth, as they both spent together.

All was still. The room was quite quiet. No sound could be heard but Fanny's sighs of pleasure, growing gradually weaker and weaker, and her father's torturous breathing as he lay heavily upon her, his eyes closed in the oblivious repose of satisfied lust.

"Well, Fan, how did you run on just now! What would your ma say if she could have heard you?"

A slight noise resounded through the room, near the fireplace, in a corner-it seemed to Sandcross who started and turned towards the screen. Fanny sat up and her glance followed that of her father.

The flimsy barrier fell, and Fanny's mother stood stiffly erect. In one hand she held her little bottle and reticule; the other was stretched out towards her naked husband and daughter. Although the room was nearly dark, Mrs. Sandcross's white face and staring blue eyes, showing a vast and terrifying dilatation like unto mother-o'-pearl round the pupils, gleamed out against the blackness of the shadows as if the features were illumined from within, and lighted up the space immediately surrounding her mask of agony.

"You vile wretches" she gasped out, in hoarse tones-almost like those of a man. "Curse you both! May you- I-I-oh!"

A long, low, painful sigh came from the innermost depths of her panting breast, and she dropped back in the armchair. Her eyes closed peacefully. All anger left her face. She was still, reposing, as it appeared, after the great shock.

"Oh, pa! She's fainted," whispered the nude daughter, catching up her petticoat, by an automatic movement of long-forgotten pudicity in the presence of her mother.

Sandcross stepped forward, placing his hand on his wife's shoulder, and gazing intently into her face. All at once, he started back.

"No, Fanny. She's dead!"

The verdict was heart failure. The joyous emotion of meeting a beloved husband and dutiful daughter when still weak from prolonged illness had been too much for her. All her lady friends envied her painless, sudden, happy death in the arms of the loved ones to whom she had just been reunited.

Fanny and her father are perfectly and unreservedly happy. They never leave each other. If you are fond of visiting Parisian playhouses, on subscribers' nights, or on the second or third performance of a new piece, you cannot forego having the beautiful Miss Sandcross pointed out to you.

You will know her by the wondering infantile simplicity in the candid glance of her violet eyes. She wears a magnificent ruby and diamond brooch, in which is set a most artistic little miniature of her doting father, whom you will notice always seated behind her in the private box, and supping with her afterwards.

THE END

Made in United States
North Haven, CT
20 December 2021

13335006R10069